Interference

Married to the Game, Volume 2

Sherron Elise

Published by Sherron Elise, 2023.

Also by Sherron Elise

Married to the Game
Interference
Game Time

The Slumber Sisters
Think Fast
So Many Secrets
My Sisters' Keeper
The Christmas Wish
Differences
Crush
Copycat

Standalone
A Kiss From An Angel
All That Glitters
Rumorz
The Baby on the Doorstep
The Desire of Her Heart
The College Christian Chat 21 Day Devotional
Excess Baggage

SECOND QUARTER

Chapter One

Tatum Watts sat in the rear seat of the chauffeured black Escalade, trying her best to ignore the paparazzi and the flashes from their cameras as they surrounded the vehicle hurling questions as they tried to get a shot of Tatum through the tinted windows. The attorney assured her that King's return to New York City would be discreet, but Tatum should've known news would leak to these bloodthirsty camera crews and news reporters. Her husband, King, had posted a seventy-five-thousand-dollar bail and was being escorted back to the city on a private jet. She wished he'd hurry so they could beat a speedy exit away from the annoying and intrusive questions.

"Tatum, do you believe King is innocent?"

"Will you be filing for a divorce now that these allegations have come to light?"

"Is it true that you're pregnant?"

Now how in the hell did that piece of news leak? Tatum wondered, as she'd just discovered two weeks ago that they were expecting and had shared the news with no one outside of their family.

Finally Tatum spotted King striding toward the vehicle, and the reporters and paparazzi were relentless as they accosted him. King's handsome caramel-toned features were a steely mask as he kept moving forward, not acknowledging any of the questions being tossed at him. King had just reached the vehicle when a big and burly white man wearing a tan trench coat pushed his way through the media fracas. Tatum's hazel eyes widened as the man brandished a pistol and aimed it at King.

"Rapist," the man yelled before pulling the trigger.

Tatum screamed in horror as King was struck by the bullet. He then clutched his chest and fell to the ground.

Pandemonium ensued as Tatum darted out of the vehicle and tried to assist her fallen husband. Women wearing shirts with *Rapist* written on the front had sprinted forward and started to chant "Protect our women!" Tears coursed down Tatum's cheeks as she cradled King's head.

"I'm sorry, Tatum. So sorry," King muttered before a quick intake of breath. He then closed his eyes.

"You all heard him. He just apologized for the rape. He's guilty," a woman exclaimed.

"King, baby, wake up, please," Tatum screamed.

"The rapist is dead. It's what he deserves," a man's voice chimed in.

Tatum released another scream of grief and agony as she held the lifeless body of her college sweetheart in her arms.

***

Tatum bolted up in bed, gasping for breath, her eyes darting wildly around the darkened bedroom as she awakened from the terrible nightmare. She reached for her cell phone, which was charging on the bedside table and saw that it was just before daybreak. King was scheduled to return home on a private jet at the Teterboro airport. He'd spent the night in a jail in Dayton, Ohio, where he'd been booked on rape charges. King's arrest had been captured live on television, and the world was abuzz with endless commentary, speculations, and judgments.

Tatum, still shaken and disoriented from the horrible and surreal nightmare of King getting shot dead, willed herself out of bed to prepare to get ready to meet him at the airport. It came as no surprise that news media were staked out in the vicinity of the private airport for miles, hoping to catch a single glimpse of the fallen NBA hero. The skies were overcast and dreary as a misty rain fell, which was typical for early April. The weather matched the gloom within Tatum's heart.

Upon landing, King was ushered to the awaiting vehicle by his attorney, Daniel Rosenberg. Daniel got into the front seat while King joined Tatum in the back. Not a word was spoken as the driver pulled off and drove back toward their home in Manhattan.

Tatum sat stoic and mute. A part of her was put out that King didn't enter the vehicle on his knees and begging for her forgiveness, but she realized her posture more than likely insinuated her anger at him and that she wasn't in the mood for any foolishness. So perhaps it was wise of him to keep his mouth shut until they returned home.

As soon as they were in the confines of their Central Park South apartment, Tatum let King have it, beating at his broad, muscular chest in a fit of frustration, anger, and humiliation.

"Do I look like a fool to you? So this is exactly why you came home with that whole 'baby, let's get married' like you're Jagged Edge or somebody? You didn't rush this marriage for love. You rushed it because you're a selfish, egotistical bastard. Did you rape that girl, King?"

"Tatum, are you seriously asking me that? You know me. Have I ever been accused of something like this while we were at UCLA?"

"No, I don't know you at all, King 'cause the man I fell in love with wouldn't have had the gall to set foot in this house and not tell me he was facing rape charges. You didn't open your mouth about it, knowing that it was only a matter of time before you'd be charged. You know what you did instead? You whisked me off on this fairytale honeymoon to Italy to evade arrest. That's exactly why you chose to leave the country, isn't it? Tell the truth."

King dropped his head.

"I'm filing for an annulment, and since the ink is barely dry on our marriage license, the process should be rather quick."

"No, Tatum, please don't leave me. I need you. I need you to help me fight this."

"You weren't thinking about needing me when you were sleeping with that cheerleader, were you? King, I'll ask you again, did you rape her?"

"No, Tatum. It was consensual, I promise."

"So the only thing you're guilty of is cheating on me yet again?"

"Tatum, please—"

"I'm going to pack my things and head back to Houston. My attorney will be in touch."

"Wow, so you're ready to bail on this marriage at the first sign of trouble?"

"King, you bailed on this relationship as soon as we got to New York after you were drafted. I just didn't want to admit it. I'm tired of lying to myself."

"Look, if you're going to leave, can you at least wait until all of this blows over? We are going to try and reach a settlement with this girl. I'm sure all she wants is money. Man, I should've known better. I can't believe I let myself get caught up like this."

"Why are you dishing out cash if you didn't rape her? You're not going to try to beat this case in court?" Tatum asked. His willingness to settle made her once again question his innocence.

"Daniel advised me that it may be easier to just settle than risk going to trial. The jury and court system may try and make an example out of me—another black athlete caught up in something stupid. I can't take that chance, Tatum. He already told me about how I'm being crucified in the media. Daniel has gotten phone calls from companies wanting to pull my endorsements."

Tatum's heart stirred. A part of her felt sorry for King, as the dark side of fame was rearing its ugly head. Since his stellar performance at the All-Star game, companies were clamoring to sign deals with King. But now that he found himself in hot water, they were treating him like a social pariah. Tatum took a deep breath. "Okay. I'll stay and help you get through this tough time, King," she promised.

Tatum went into their bedroom, slamming the door. She was angry at herself for not standing her ground and leaving King as he deserved. She hoped this decision wouldn't come back to haunt her. She fell upon the bed, and for the umpteenth time in the past twenty-four hours, she had another good, long cry.

Chapter Two

Gya Green didn't know why she was torturing herself. Since learning of her husband, Bryant's betrayal, she'd beat a hasty retreat from their home in Miami and returned to Houston to live with her parents. Now a soon-to-be divorcee, she was back in the house she grew up in, burrowed under blankets in her old bedroom watching the video of their marriage proposal.

The evening was magical. Gya was a college senior and under the assumption she was attending a jersey retirement celebration for Bryant. She was dressed in an elegant black dress and heels for the ceremony, which was taking place on the fifty-yard line of Kyle field. She had just exited the tunnel, arm-in-arm with Bryant, and headed toward his family who was already assembled on the field. But to her surprise, her parents were present as well. The surprise continued when Gya saw the words written on the jumbotron at the end zone: *Gya, will you marry me?*

Stunned, Gya's eyes were wide with wonder as she looked at Bryant. He bent on one knee and formally asked for her hand in marriage. Gya realized the jersey retirement was nothing but a ruse orchestrated by Bryant and their families. She was a bundle of tears as she accepted his proposal and he placed the princess-cut diamond ring upon her finger. The proposal was the perfect climax to their college courtship, which began when Bryant had knocked her off her feet—literally—when they were college freshmen. She was attending cheerleader camp, and he was jogging during his football training camp when he accidentally collided into Gya. Being the sweet gentlemen he was raised as, he escorted her to their student health center, and he stayed while her scraped knee was attended to. He then walked her back to her dorm but sought her out again later that evening in the dining hall. They'd exchanged numbers and were practically inseparable from that moment on.

Now, not even a year into their marriage and nearly four months pregnant, Gya was facing the idea of life as a single mother. Bryant had betrayed her with an act of infidelity mere months into their marriage and had fathered another child, a baby girl, with a woman who was an associate of their family.

Gya bitterly watched the highlight video of their wedding. Their one-year anniversary was in two months, and instead of the trip to the Maldives they'd initially planned, they were heading to divorce court.

Gya couldn't understand where things had gone so horribly wrong. This was a life beyond her wildest nightmares. She never thought she'd be a single mother and caught up in a nasty love triangle that had social media on the edge of their seats as they awaited new developments. The horror story began when a malicious woman confronted Gya at Gya's book signing, taking evil pleasure in informing her that Bryant was the father of a new baby girl. She even went as far as showing her the photo of Bryant cradling the baby in the hospital room. Gya never identified who the woman was and figured she was some gossip blog correspondent. It didn't even matter. All that Gya fathomed was that her brand, built on her strong faith in God and female empowerment, was now an utter joke. Bryant had made a total fool of her in front of the masses. He'd initially lied and said Mercedes, the mother of his daughter, fabricated her pregnancy, but he'd merely paid her hush money to recant. It then leaked that she'd given birth.

The National Football League had seemed to change Bryant's personality from that of a southern gentleman to a deceitful snake she didn't recognize. And things weren't faring well for her cousin, Tatum, either. Gya could hardly believe it when her mother informed her that Tatum's husband, King, had been arrested for rape. It now appeared that her marriage wasn't the only one that would be short-lived. Gya and Tatum had endured a roller coaster of crazy situations since embarking on this journey of being married to sports superstars, and it seemed like the ride was only getting rougher. But Gya had finally had enough and was screaming to get off.

Chapter Three

Tatum's features were taut and aloof as she sat on the living room sofa flanked by King; his father and business manager, Jacoby; King's attorney, Daniel; and his publicist Kimberly Shaw, as they tried to come up with a game plan of handling the media firestorm that was engulfing King day by day.

"King, I need you to lay out the facts for us now that we're all present. Of course I've heard your statement, but we need to be on one accord for the press conference," Daniel said.

Tatum's stomach lurched at the words *press conference* as she wasn't relishing presenting a united front and sitting beside King as hundreds of cameras and reporters stared them in their faces.

"Well, during the championship game, I noticed one of the cheerleaders kept giving me the eye, so after the game I approached her, and we struck up a conversation. I invited her to my hotel room, and of course she took me up on the offer."

"King, the police report filed says her cheerleading uniform was ripped," the publicist, Kimberly, spoke up.

"Yes, I admit I ripped it off her while we were in the heat of the moment."

Tatum exhaled loudly, trying her best not to lunge at King. The rumbling within her stomach would rate as a ten on the Richter scale. She didn't know if the nausea she experienced daily was a result of her pregnancy or if it was stress-induced anxiety and nerves from the ordeal she and King were embroiled in. But given how her stomach roared with each sickening detail of King's illicit tryst, she fathomed it was stress.

"I'm sorry, Tay. I know this is hard," King said, his eyes contrite.

Tatum rolled her own eyes at him in turn, sick of his lame apologies.

King hesitated for a few moments before he continued to spill the rest of the sordid tale. "After the girl and I had sex, I asked her did she want to shower, and she said no. I realize now it was all part of her plan. She didn't want to wash away any supposed evidence that would give credence to her lies."

"So you didn't use a condom?" Kimberly pressed.

"No. I didn't have any on me."

"As you shouldn't. You're a married man, King, but that didn't stop you from getting yours, did it?" Tatum said. *Or taking it*, she thought, still not fully convinced of his innocence.

"Let's move on to the details of the press conference," Kimberly intervened. "It will be televised live, that way we don't have to worry about the media placing their own spin on your words, King. Tatum's either."

Tatum's eyes darted in her direction. "My words? I'm not saying anything."

"Okay, that's fine," Kimberly agreed, "and actually King's speaking will be very limited. We're not allowing him to take any questions from the press. The main purpose of the press conference is to lay out the facts and have King proclaim his innocence, along with an apology to the Flash coaches and staff, his teammates, and his fans."

Tatum had to keep from laughing in derision. She was the only person he needed to apologize to as far as she was concerned.

After everyone left and King went into the kitchen to fix something to eat, Tatum decided to reach out to her friend, Kelsea West, who was the wife of King's teammate, Antoine.

"Hey, girl. I can imagine how you feel right now. I'm sorry for not reaching out sooner, but I wanted to give you your space and time to process everything. Not only that, but Ariana is upset at the possibility of Russell being traded since he's a free agent. From what Antoine told me, a trade is inevitable for him since he's nearing veteran status and not as fast as he used to be. Wesley Johnson is set to be traded as well," Kelsea said.

Ariana was their other good friend, and the trio had grown close since Tatum had first moved to New York City. But Wesley was nothing but a nuisance to the Flash organization, as well as a nemesis of King's, so Tatum was glad he was on the trading block.

"I'd really miss Ariana," Tatum said.

"And I'm going to miss you. Who did you hire to handle the annulment?" Kelsea asked.

"I'm not leaving King just yet," Tatum replied.

"What?" Kelsea said, incredulous. "Tatum, surely you're not staying married to a rapist. I mean him giving you the STD a while back was one thing. I encouraged you to give him another chance after that, but not this time."

"Kelsea, we don't know that King has raped that girl. It's her word against his, and I'm choosing to believe my husband," Tatum said, her words belying her earlier doubts of his innocence.

"You're choosing to be a fool, Tatum, and Antoine said he plans to be present at the press conference tomorrow to support King even though I begged him not to. I don't want him to get entangled in this mess and have fans start withdrawing their support of him too."

"Antoine is standing by King's side as any real friend would, and I thought you would have my back too."

"Look, I never told you this, but I was almost raped in college while out on a date, so this hits close to home for me. I mean, I guess I should refrain from further judgment until King is tried in the court of law, but I'm not gonna lie: I have my reservations."

Tatum sighed. "I'm sorry to hear about what happened to you, and I guess I have no choice but to respect your stance."

Tatum hung up with a heavy heart. So many people were divided against King, and now she found herself caught in the middle, as it seemed people were willing to turn against her, too, for standing by her man.

***

"I want the city of New York as well as the world to know that I am innocent of these charges. The only thing I am guilty of is the act of infidelity against my wife whom I love dearly. I deeply apologize to my wife, my parents and brother, along with the Flash organization and my teammates, as well as to all my fans. I know I let a lot of people down," King said, his voice low and monotone as he spoke into the mic the following day at the press conference held at the Pat Riley arena. Tatum sat at his side, and he clasped her hand and brought it to his lips. "You're my rib, and I thank you for standing by my side. I've been in love with you since our freshman year of college. I know I don't deserve you, and I vow to spend the rest of my life making this up to you."

Daniel stood and thanked the press for coming, gesturing for King and Tatum to stand and make their exit, amid reporters firing questions at them in their wake.

"King, do you feel your actions have served as a distraction to the Baylor Bears and their championship win? Do you want to apologize to the team?"

"Tatum, are you going to leave King? Do you accept his apology?"

"King, will you and Bryant Green seek family counseling together to restore your marriages?"

Tatum tuned out all of the asinine questions being hurled at them by the media. She blinked back tears of anger, hurt, and humiliation as they left the press conference area. Tatum wasn't moved by King's words because he'd made loads of empty promises since their move to New York. Yes, he'd cheated before, but it had never become a public spectacle. King was right. It would take a lifetime for her to forgive him for this latest transgression.

Chapter Four

It was now mid-May, and Gya was stir crazy. Embarrassment kept her confined to her childhood home, and her mother, Pam, thought it would be best if she limited her activity. Her mother had concerns that Gya would endure another miscarriage. This was compounded by Gya being tagged or alerted online to some new salacious story concerning Bryant and their love triangle.

But for Gya, something had to give because her grandmother always said an idle mind was the devil's workshop. Her words couldn't be truer because Gya's anger at Bryant deepened day after day, even in the midst of his relentless texts and phone calls.

"Some of my teammates suggested I give you time and space, but Gya it's been torture for me not to be able to hold and kiss you each night. The bed feels so cold and empty without you, bae. I love and miss you so much, and I can't say enough how sorry I am for hurting you like I did."

Gya was silent on the other end of the line, which compelled Bryant to continue. "If you're unsure of anything, please know this: I have not been with any other women since sleeping with Mercedes, and I only paid her hush money to protect our marriage. Can't you understand I tried my best to conceal her pregnancy because of how much I love you?"

"Bryant, no excuses will make what you did right. How long did you think you could get away with hiding your secret love child from me? The truth always comes to light, and it exploded in both of our faces. I didn't deserve to be hurt like this. I tried my best to be a great wife to you." Gya's voice choked up with tears.

Bryant released a groan of agony. "It's killing me to know you're hurting like this, and I'm the cause of it. I hate not being able to console you."

"I don't want you anywhere near me. Your touch wouldn't be welcomed or appreciated," Gya said, her words and tone filled with frustration and disdain.

"Gya, I wasn't trying to be malicious in hiding the pregnancy. Honestly, I wasn't even thinking straight. I was so afraid of losing you that I wasn't rational in my actions. But what I feared the most has happened. I know I deserve it, but I wish you would just take a little more time and realize we can work this out."

"So you want me to accept your outside child? I would only resent her, Bryant, and that's not fair to her. She didn't ask to be born. And I wouldn't dare be selfish enough to request that you shun her and not acknowledge her existence."

"You're right, and I wouldn't. I do plan on manning up and doing the right thing by being an active part of her life."

His words tore Gya to her core, although she would expect nothing less of him. Yet it still hurt to know another woman gave him a child before she did.

"As you should. Goodbye, Bryant. You'll be hearing from my attorney soon to start the divorce proceedings. Please stop calling me. All further conversation and contact can be handled through our lawyers." With those final parting words, Gya hung up.

She tried to keep her thoughts off Bryant and their impending divorce by watching shows on Hallmark and Lifetime, although Hallmark seemed to be the safer bet. Lifetime had her plotting all kinds of dangerous demises for Bryant. But after a while, she got tired of the sappy love stories and happy endings of Hallmark movies. Love was nothing but a big joke, and she couldn't believe she was once naïve enough to believe in fairytale marriages.

When not watching television, she had old school R&B songs on shuffle via her Apple Music playlist. It was like a dagger to her heart when Tevin Campbell's "Can We Talk" began to play, as it was a song Bryant attempted to sing to her when he first asked her out, and she almost found herself laughing at how off-key his voice was. She quickly suppressed the memory and clicked off the song. But she kept Toni Braxton's song "Stupid" on repeat because she felt like the biggest fool of them all.

Gya could recall how she used to fill her days creating vlogs and going live on Instagram for Bible studies and random conversations with her followers. Now she had become the audience, as she enjoyed watching other inspirational YouTubers such as the anointed prophetess and psalmist Hannah Heals who was based out of Atlanta. Gya had discovered Hannah's ministry shortly after her first miscarriage last year. Hannah often shared her own testimony of being barren and God opening her womb and blessing her with three children. Her spiritual videos were a great source of encouragement to Gya, and she was excited to learn that Hannah would be ministering in Houston the following week at the Fountain of Praise church. Gya purchased a ticket for herself and for her mom who was glad to accompany Gya, as she had become worried when Gya shied away from attending church. Yes, Gya still called herself being salty at God for allowing her to look like a grade-A clown to the masses. It was also difficult to attend her childhood church now that she was back in Houston. It was the same church in which she'd wed Bryant, and she didn't want to return, envisioning herself as a bride all those months ago as Bryant awaited to take her hand when she reached the altar, his eyes glistening with tears at the sight of his breathtaking bride.

Gya shared this with her mom as they drove to the Fountain of Praise, rubbing her belly as her mother steered her Mercedes coupe down the Sam Houston South Tollway.

"Mom, I always wanted my children to grow up in a loving two-parent household. I hate I won't be able to give my child that, especially when I was able to experience it. I feel like I've already failed as a parent."

"Gya, you had no control over Bryant's actions. Trust me, God will take care of you and this child, and you know your father and I plan to love and spoil the baby endlessly. Just like your dad has been spoiling you since you've been back home," Pam said, playfully cutting her eyes at Gya. "But you'd better cut back on those turkey legs because all of that sodium content can't be good for you or the baby."

Gya's pregnancy craving was the shrimp alfredo stuffed turkey leg from Houston's famed Turkey Leg Hut. Being as how the restaurant wasn't located too far from the medical center, Gya's father stopped and picked her up one weekly after leaving his job as a cardiologist.

Once arriving at the Fountain of Praise and heading inside, they saw a live worship team performing as all attendees were coming in and getting seated. Gya couldn't help but sway and clap along to the music. She realized she'd missed the church atmosphere more than she'd thought.

Soon, Hannah Heals took center stage with her beautiful and smooth voice, singing a rendition of "The Goodness of God." Gya found herself becoming emotional as the lyrics penetrated her heart and mind. In spite of it all, God had been so faithful to her, but she'd turned her back on him at the first sign of trouble. Where was *her* faithfulness?

After rendering a few more songs, Hannah began to go forth in the prophetic, walking the aisles and praying over different people in the audience as she gave them utterances from God. Hannah then did an altar call for all women in the audience who were expecting or hoping to conceive. At that point Hannah and Gya locked eyes, and Gya thought she would lose it when Hannah strode to her row and clasped her hand. She summoned for Gya to get up and join her at the altar.

"God wants you to stop being a coward," Hannah said, and Gya was bawling before Hannah could finish the sentence. "He wants you to stop trying to take the easy way out."

Gya knew exactly what Hannah was referring to. It was something she hadn't uttered to anyone, not even her mother. Gya had contemplated aborting her child, but it was so egregious that she tried to push the thought away. It was hard to admit that a selfish part of her wanted to get rid of the child because she wanted no further ties to Bryant, and she didn't want her child having to share a father with his illegitimate daughter. Abortion was illegal in the state of Texas, but Gya pondered traveling to New York or California and discreetly having the procedure performed. She was ashamed that the thought of hurting Bryant by going behind his back and aborting their child gave her a sick form of pleasure. But now God had allowed for Hannah's prophetic gifting to read her like a book.

Hannah shared the next prophetic utterance with Gya privately, whispering in her ear and not talking into the mic.

"You're thinking about writing another book, this time for divorced women. You are even considering starting a ministry to help divorced women. While your actions would be noble, you cannot minister to others from a broken place. You are pouring from an empty cup, and since you're hurting, you can't effectively minister to others. You could do more damage than good. Put all thoughts of ministry aside until you heal from the bitterness that has taken root. You are the one who needs ministering to at this point."

Gya stretched her hands in the air as Hannah prayed over her that healing and forgiveness could go forth. She also laid hands on Gya's womb and prayed for her unborn child. Gya was a mess of tears as she gave Hannah the biggest bear hug once she was done.

"You don't know how much I needed this, how much you've blessed me. I'm so glad I came tonight," Gya said, sobbing.

"Yes, God knew exactly what you needed. He's an awesome God. Now go in peace," Hannah encouraged.

Once returning to take her seat, she saw her mom was in tears too. "Looks like you got a breakthrough tonight, Gya. It was so hard to see you in such a broken place. I pray it's only uphill from here."

"Yes, I strongly believe it is. I'm ready to get out of my spiritual funk and start living again. No more pity parties. It's time to take my life back. It's time to heal," Gya agreed.

***

The following week, Pam accompanied Gya to her doctor's appointment where Gya would find out the gender of her child. Gya had initially planned to have a gender reveal party when she first learned of her pregnancy, but the drama with Bryant had caused all excitement about the pregnancy to temporarily wane. Her mother still suggested having a gender reveal with a small gathering of family and friends, but Gya declined.

She couldn't believe her eyes when they pulled up to the medical building, and she spotted Bryant.

Gya got out of the car on a rampage. "What the hell are you doing here, Bryant?" she said as she accosted him. "Didn't I tell you I didn't want anything else to do with you during our last conversation? How did you even know I'd be here?"

"Now Gya, calm down. I'm the one who told him. In spite of how you might feel about him, this is still his child, and I felt he had the right to be present when you found out the gender," her mother explained.

"Mom, I don't want him here. Bryant, please leave."

Bryant adamantly shook his head. "Like your mother said, Gya, this is my child too. I realize you hate my guts—and rightfully so I might add—but just like with my daughter, I plan to be a part of this child's life every step of the way, starting with attending all doctor visits when I can."

"Just shut up and leave me alone." Gya turned and waddled into the building, shooing Bryant away as he tried to hold the door open for her. She ignored him as they awaited the elevator to take them to the OB/GYN floor. Gya exhaled long and hard in annoyance when Bryant took a seat directly next to her. Her face was a mask of stone as they sat in the waiting area. She stared straight ahead, awaiting to be summoned to the examination room. When her name was finally called and Bryant stood and grabbed her hand, Gya snatched it away as if Bryant's touch was a coal of fire.

"You two go on back. I'll wait out here," Pam said.

"Mom, I wanted you to be present when I learn the gender," Gya whined.

"Gya, just go," Pam instructed.

A nurse took her weight and blood pressure. Gya imagined that the nurse and her OB/GYN, Dr. Nolan, could sense the tension between her and Bryant. But the doctor chattered excitedly as she rubbed the cold gel on Gya's abdomen. She rolled the wand around, and Gya could hear the strength of her child's heartbeat.

"Looks like we have us a baby boy," Dr. Nolan announced.

"Yes," Bryant exclaimed.

Gya glared at him and his nerve. This should've been a much happier occasion where they could celebrate together, but his presence was sullying the moment for her.

The doctor helped Gya sit up, giving her a napkin to wipe the gel off her belly. Gya straightened her clothing and listened as Dr. Nolan gave details for her next appointment in a few weeks. Gya thanked her, Bryant followed suit, and he trailed Gya out of the examination room.

"Gya, I was hoping we'd be able to talk," Bryant said as they entered the waiting area where Pam sat reading a magazine. She looked up in expectancy.

"It's a boy, Mom," Gya announced.

Pam smiled. "My first grandson. Wait until I tell your father. He's always wanted a boy." Due to Pam suffering from endometriosis, conception after Gya had been difficult.

Bryant trailed them out to the parking lot to Pam's car. Bryant halted Gya right as she opened the passenger-side door. "Gya, I really need to talk to you."

Gya slammed the door and whirled around to face him. "What, Bryant? What do you want? Haven't you already done enough to make me miserable? Why can't you just go away and leave me alone?"

"Why haven't you filed for divorce yet, Gya?"

"Oh, don't worry I plan to. My main concern when I first found out about your deceit is getting the hell away from you. You'll be hearing from my attorney real soon."

"I was hoping you haven't filed because you were willing to think things through and not give up on our marriage."

"Did you suffer some type of concussion recently I don't know about? 'Cause you're talking real crazy right now. I was foolish enough to give you another chance when we first learned Mercedes was pregnant—when you had the audacity to sit in my face and lie, telling me she recanted her story and wasn't even pregnant."

"I never said she wasn't pregnant, Gya, just that she recanted."

"All prodded in part by *you*. A lie is a lie, Bryant. Look, just leave me alone. I don't want you at any more of my doctor's appointments. I will notify you when I'm in labor."

"No way. You can't shut me out like this, Gya. This is my son you're carrying, and I want to be there every step of the way. I'm no deadbeat."

"Go focus on your daughter with Mercedes. What's her name anyway?"

"Brelynn."

"Wow, she even had the nerve to give her a name similar to yours. You know what, let me go ahead and give you this divorce so you and Mercedes can embark on your new lives together as one big happy family with *Brelynn*."

"I have no intentions or interest in marrying Mercedes. Hell, I don't even like her to be honest."

Gya laughed uproariously. "You liked her enough to sleep with her and knock her up. You sound pathetic. Like I said, just leave me alone, Bryant."

Gya got into the car without a backward glance at him. As her mom drove away, Gya felt consumed with jealousy, and the name Brelynn kept reverberating in her mind. Her son would have to share his father with a child Gya couldn't help but resent. It wasn't fair. She should've been the only mother to Bryant's kids. She'd always found baby mama scenarios to be so ratchet and now she found herself caught up in one. Ooh, she could kill Bryant for putting her in this type of predicament. The devil was so cunning. She'd been on such a high since Hannah had prayed for her, but encountering Bryant caused all the rage and anger to course through her once again. Would she ever be able to fully heal and forgive?

Chapter Five

Gya was astonished when Hannah reached out to her through DM on Instagram, providing her phone number and requesting that Gya call her. Gya immediately complied.

"Honestly, you've been in my prayers since the entire scandal with your husband first broke. Like you said, it was divine intervention that brought you to my event in Houston. God has had you on my heart since I encountered you, and I feel He is pressing upon me to be your spiritual mentor and help you heal," Hannah said.

"Oh wow, I'd love that, Hannah. It would be an honor to have you mentor me," Gya said.

"I hope I'm not being too forward by stating this, but as a prophetess, being blunt is second nature for me. Anyhow, I feel the reason why your ministry took such a drastic turn is because you didn't have the proper guidance. You're still so young and have a lot to learn, and I'm going to teach you everything I can. I would like for you to come to Atlanta for the summer and shadow me in my ministry and church. I'm even willing to cover your hotel fee and all expenses for the duration of your stay. The Westin Hotel in Buckhead has a great spa, and I'm sure you could use some pregnancy pampering. I can also connect you with a great gynecologist for your pregnancy checkups while you're here."

Gya's eyes and spirits brightened even more. "I'd love that, Hannah. Wow. I can't thank you enough for this."

"Okay, I'll be in touch so we can finalize the details," Hannah said.

Gya immediately went downstairs and filled her mom in about her plans for a temporary move to Atlanta.

"I was more comfortable with you being here with your father and me so we could monitor your pregnancy. Are you sure this won't place any stress on you and Landon?" Pam asked, already calling her grandson by the name Gya had decided on. Gya knew Bryant always wanted a junior, but she'd always loved the name Landon, and she had to admit to herself she was being spiteful by not naming him Bryant, Jr.

"I'll be fine, Mom. Besides, Hannah mentioned treating me to day spa visits. I can hardly wait. I needed something to brighten my spirits, and this is definitely a start. And you know her ministry revolves around praying for and nurturing pregnant women. I feel that I am in more-than-capable hands."

"Well, that's good to hear. So long as you're okay with it, then I'm onboard too. But I'll miss you. I'd gotten used to having my baby back at home."

Gya smiled and kissed her mom's cheek. "I know one thing. I want one more turkey leg before I leave Houston."

They both shared a laugh and made plans to do some shopping for summer maternity clothes for Gya to tote along to the ATL. Gya had high hopes that this trip was the beginning of her spiritual renewal.

Chapter Six

In a scene reminiscent of her first nightmare surrounding King's arrest, Tatum found herself in the midst of a media frenzy as their black SUV pulled up to the courthouse in Dayton, Ohio. It was a Thursday morning on the last week of May, which marked King's initial court appearance, and reporters swarmed the vehicle like ravenous killer bees. Tatum could already hear the questions being hurled as she took in the sight of several television satellite trucks that lined the street in front of the courthouse. Reporters, photographers, fans, and protesters had come out in droves, hoping to catch a live glimpse of the NBA's disgraced player.

"Remember, once we exit the vehicle, stare straight ahead. Do not answer any questions," King's attorney Daniel coached.

Tatum had to refrain from rolling her eyes, as she didn't need any reminders not to talk to the bloodthirsty media. She was becoming engulfed in the madness, and she wanted it to end, but sadly, this was only the beginning.

Tatum gritted her teeth as she grabbed King's hand, and they strode toward the doors of the courthouse. She didn't like the ruse of this united front, but Daniel and the publicist Kimberly kept insisting it would help King's cause in the eyes of the general public. But fans and protesters alike yelled in their direction as they continued on what Tatum viewed as a perp walk.

"We love you, King."

"We know you're innocent."

"You're a rapist, King. I hope you're found guilty."

"We must fight to protect women."

To Tatum's further annoyance, there were just as many reporters and photographers packed inside of the courtroom, lining the rear wall. Even though Daniel had stated the accuser wouldn't be present for this hearing, Tatum's sharp hazel eyes did a cursory sweep around the courtroom, wondering if she'd changed her mind. But there was no sign of her. Her identity continued to be withheld from the public, and Daniel revealed that she feared for her safety given that King was still a beloved public figure by many.

Although the woman's identity was a secret from the public, Tatum had received her name through Daniel as he'd read from the police report. Tatum reached out to the private investigator she'd hired to trail King in the latter part of the previous year. The same PI uncovered King's ongoing affair with an Instagram model by the name of Ireland. The same IG model who'd had the gall to sneak past building security and confront Tatum at their apartment, taunting her about her clandestine relationship with King. Well the PI gave Tatum further details about his accuser, a junior student at Baylor University named Whitney Prescott. She'd even provided photos of the beautiful blond cheerleader with the translucent ocean blue eyes.

Tatum's imagination ran wild as she imagined this Whitney in the throes of passion with her husband because given his claim of it being consensual, she imagined them having rough and rowdy sex. Then Whitney's face morphed into Ireland's, followed by the thoughts of the countless other women King probably kept company with behind her back. The faceless women who'd had a piece of her husband. Tatum shuddered at the thought of her husband being community property.

"You cold, baby?" King asked, attempting to place an arm around her shoulders.

Tatum abruptly dodged his arm and shot him a look of death but then remembered the many reporters and cameras present. Tatum was tired of the pretenses, and she got a sense of satisfaction at the crestfallen look on King's face at her rejection.

Tatum took her seat within the audience while King sat up front with his lawyer. She couldn't believe there was such a media raucous for a hearing that didn't last more than ten minutes. King's voice was as low and monotone as it had been during the press conference as he answered the judge's questions with a "yes, sir" or "no, sir." Before ending the hearing, the judge instated a gag order on all parties involved, including Tatum. It was made clear that Daniel, King, nor Tatum could discuss any aspect of the case in the media. The same restrictions would apply to Whitney. The preliminary hearing that would determine whether or not the case would go to trial was scheduled for July. Tatum had to restrain from releasing a laugh of derision at the irony. July was the month they'd originally planned to get married. Instead of their dream wedding, King would be facing the possibility of prison time.

Tatum was relieved when court was adjourned and they walked to their vehicle to return to the airport and board the private jet that would transport them back to New York. With the preliminary hearing two months away, Tatum didn't relish the agony of awaiting King's fate. The joy of her pregnancy was marred by this rape case debacle. She missed the days when she was just a carefree cheerleader at UCLA. She hated to admit it, but if she could do it all over again, Tatum would've never accepted King's offer of a first date. She had no idea as a naïve college freshman that what began as a fairytale courtship would turn into a sordid tabloid-worthy drama. King had gotten their lives entangled in this foolishness, and Tatum was being dragged in the court of public opinion for deciding to stick by her man. As far as she was concerned, her only crime was falling in love.

Chapter Seven

On a Monday evening in early June, Gya's temporary move to Atlanta was complete, and she was all settled in to her suite at the Westin Buckhead. Hannah came to the hotel to greet and welcome Gya to the city and then transported them to a restaurant called Bar Vegan ATL for dinner so they could become better acquainted.

"I'm happy to be here in Atlanta, although June is a bit of a bittersweet month for me because the purity conference I had planned was supposed to be taking place this month."

Hannah raised an eyebrow. "Purity conference?"

Gya explained how she planned to have high school– and college-aged girls dressed in white ball gowns and be presented with purity rings as they committed to remain virgins until marriage. Gya even had a sponsorship with the retailer Claire's, but it was pulled once the conference was canceled.

"Anyway, I'm so excited to try this place. I can't wait to check out the sister restaurant, Slutty Vegan, while I'm here in Atlanta too."

"Yes, it's just as delicious," Hannah assured. "I'm so glad you're here, and once we place our orders I want to share with you some further instructions God has for you."

Gya ordered a Cheesesteak Eggrollz combo that included tater tots while Hannah requested the Fried Chik'n sandwich.

"God wants you to pull away from social media completely while you're in Atlanta. I'm talking a complete detox," Hannah said.

Gya nodded and took a sip of the strawberry lemonade the waitress had just placed in front of her. "I'm in full agreement on that. I'm tired of being pinged in notifications that involve yet another smut story written about me or Bryant. I've had about all I can take of my cousin Tatum's drama as well. And you won't believe this, but the girl my husband fathered a child with even had the nerve to DM me, taunting me with foolishness. I immediately blocked her."

Hannah's beautiful brown eyes widened. "What did she say?"

"She cattily asked me if I wanted her to save her daughter's clothing to pass along to my child. She's so ignorant and unaware that I'm having a boy. It's bad enough that she caroused with my husband, but now to rub my face in it? She's classless."

Hannah nodded in understanding. "This Mercedes chick is operating under the Peninnah spirit. Peninnah is the woman that taunted Hannah in the book of first Samuel, when Hannah was unable to conceive a child with her husband, Elkanah. Peninnah was Elkanah's concubine who was able to birth him multiple children while Hannah was barren. Trust me, given that I'm Hannah's namesake, I know this story within the Bible like the back of my hand. You did well in blocking this girl, and it's further confirmation of God wanting you to pull away from social media. Also I have my own Peninnah story to share with you."

Hannah went on to share her testimony with Gya, relaying how like Gya, she met her husband in college at Morgan State University. "We wed about two years after graduation, but I had trouble conceiving. I became overwhelmed because fertility treatments were so expensive, so I began to pray fervently for God to open my womb. In the midst of my fertility challenges, an ex-girlfriend of Shawn's used to take pleasure in taunting me. She'd say things like had Shawn married her instead of me he'd have a houseful of kids by now, and this was God's punishment for him choosing me over her. It was a very hurtful time, but God is so faithful. He blessed me with my beautiful twin boys after several miscarriages. He definitely gave me double for my trouble. I suffered two more miscarriages after their birth, and then God blessed me with my daughter, Reagan. I'm now thirty-five, but I haven't ruled out having any more kids. God calls for us to be fruitful and multiply, and I welcome as many children as He decides to bless Shawn and me with."

"Wow. That testimony is amazing," Gya said.

Hannah's difficulty in conceiving made her feel guilty about considering aborting her child. She confided this to Hannah, telling her that she'd hit the nail on the head that night she'd prophesied to her.

Hannah patted her hand. "God is so good. Glad you didn't go through with it."

Gya and Hannah continued to engage in lighthearted conversation once their entrees arrived and then Hannah gave her a brief rundown of her church,

The Living Word, which she and her husband, Shawn, had founded five years ago, shortly after the birth of their daughter. Hannah's media following had caused the church to grow exponentially. Gya enjoyed watching the livestream services while in Houston, and she couldn't wait to attend service in person the following week.

***

Her first service at The Living Word was everything she imagined, from the high-spirited praise-and-worship team to the awesome word Shawn and Hannah rendered. Gya liked and appreciated that Hannah and her husband performed a tag team ministry in which they would deliver the sermon every Sunday together. Gya recalled reading controversial comments by some male ministers that stated that Hannah and Shawn were out of order and that God didn't ordain for women to preach alongside their husbands. Gya was glad that Hannah continued to tune out the naysayers and their traditionalistic views, allowing God to use her however He saw fit.

After church, Gya was invited to a soul food Sunday feast at Hannah and Shawn's Buckhead mansion. Gya was impressed by the beautiful home, as it looked like something from an episode of *The Real Housewives of Atlanta*.

"Caleb and Christian, stop running around this house and have a seat," Hannah admonished her eight-year old twin sons.

"No way, Mom. I'm gonna show Caleb he's not faster than me," Christian tossed over his shoulder as he continued in pursuit of his brother. The various servers had to dodge the rambunctious duo as they set out and arranged the numerous platters of food.

Hannah's six-year-old daughter, Reagan, started to pick food off the trays. Gya was surprised no one corrected the little girl about such an unsanitary practice. The behavior of Hannah's children was a bit disconcerting as they always seemed so well mannered and behaved from what Hannah shared of her family on social media.

Shawn came to bless the food, and all the guests began to dig in. After dinner, when everyone was seated in the family room having a post-dinner dessert of delicious pound cake, Gya noticed Hannah's personal assistant, Jasmin, enter carrying a box of rings from Claire's.

"Where did Hannah run off to? I have the rings she ordered for the purity conference," Jasmin said.

Gya raised an eyebrow. "Purity conference?"

"Yes. Hannah and our team are working on an awesome idea for the high school– and college-aged girls within our church congregation. We are going to purchase wedding dresses from boutiques for all of the girls who register, and they will be presented with these purity rings during the ceremony. It's going to be like a holy debutante ball."

Gya looked at Hannah questioningly when she returned to the family room from taking a phone call. "*Ahhh,* I see the rings have come in. Thanks, Jasmin. That's why I'm so glad you're here, Gya. We can greatly use your help in planning and orchestrating this conference for our young ladies at The Living Word."

Gya waited for Hannah to explain to all present that the purity conference had been her idea to begin with, but Hannah just continued to talk to her and Jasmin about further details she wanted implemented.

Gya felt herself growing angry but tried to brush it off, feeling that she was being silly. Maybe Hannah hadn't meant to blatantly steal her idea, and this was her way of salvaging an opportunity Gya felt she'd lost. So Gya put on a tight-lipped smile as Hannah continued to discuss her vision for the conference.

Caleb and Christian were now throwing a football around the house, and it nearly broke a beautiful crystal vase that rested on a glass end table.

"Shawn, can you please do something with your sons? They're in my way," Hannah said, her voice and features tight with exasperation.

"Where's Erinn? Isn't that what's she here for?" Shawn snapped back.

Erinn, the young nanny, ran in. "I'm so sorry, Pastor Shawn. I was just helping Reagan put the finishing touches on a fun craft activity we were working on. Boys, go get your swim trunks on so you can get into the pool like I promised."

This was all the twins needed to hear, and they excitedly bounced up the long, curving staircase to get changed.

Gya joined Erinn while she was outside in the backyard monitoring the boys. They were playing and splashing around in a lagoon-style pool complete with a flowing waterfall.

"They're a handful, huh? You definitely earn your paycheck," Gya remarked, only half joking.

"Oh, I don't get paid for this. I enjoy doing it," Erinn said with a smile.

Gya frowned. "You don't get paid as a nanny?"

"Oh, no, I render this service as onto the Lord. And besides, Hannah assured me this is great practice for the husband and children I'm praying to have one day," Erinn said. "Hey, Caleb, get back over to the shallow end." Erinn waited until Caleb did as she instructed before continuing. "Besides, I want to show Hannah and Shawn that I'm nothing like the last nanny. She quit and badmouthed them and the kids to people, stating that the kids were too unruly and bad behaved."

No lies detected, Gya thought.

"That's why Hannah now insists on NDAs being signed by all staff. Have you signed one?" Erinn asked.

"I'm not really considered her staff," Gya said. *And neither are you because staff should be paid,* Gya thought. "She's mentoring me, but it's nothing like an official role that would require contracts."

Gya was all too happy when Hannah drove her back to her hotel later that evening. Hannah made small talk during the drive, but Gya had too much on her mind to be really engaged in conversation. Once back inside of her hotel room, she tried to process all that had taken place that afternoon. Her mother had always said that the best way to get to really know a person was to go home with them. How right she was. Gya called her mother to unload all that had taken place.

"She stole your idea? I don't believe this, Gya."

"Yeah, I know, but I didn't want to be petty and speak up about it."

"Oh, no, you definitely need to say something, and I'm a bit disappointed that she would gaslight her nanny like that and get that poor girl to deal with those children for free. That's taking advantage of people. Not Christlike at all. See, I knew I had my reservations about you going to Atlanta."

"I don't want this one afternoon to make me regret my decision, Mom, but I will have a talk with Hannah. Wow, as a matter of fact this is her beeping in on the other line now. Let me see what she wants. I love you."

Pam returned the sentiment to her daughter, and Gya answered Hannah's call.

"Hi, Gya. I couldn't help but notice you were quiet on the way home. Look, I'm not even going to act obtuse. I know you're upset about the purity conference, but it was actually supposed to be a surprise. I know how disappointed you were about not being in the right frame of mind to host your own, so I wanted us both to work on it together. Jasmin wasn't supposed to bring out the rings today until I had a chance to talk to you, but that was my fault—simple miscommunication on my part. I do apologize. I never want you to think I'm trying to be underhanded or shady."

Gya instantly felt better. "Okay. I now totally understand, and I appreciate you setting the record straight."

"Great. What I'd love to have you do this week is reach out to local bridal shops and try to secure donations for dresses. I'm sure your marketing degree can be put to good use."

"Most definitely. Will do," Gya promised.

Once hanging up Gya prepared to take a shower and turn in for the night. Now that the air was clear, Gya still learned a valuable lesson, and that was learning to keep all future ideas and plans to herself.

Chapter Eight

As if the rape debacle couldn't grow any worse, King received word that his accuser, Whitney, had rejected his offer for a settlement. She filed a civil suit on top of the assault case. It was at that moment that Tatum felt the full magnitude of what she and her husband were up against. And just when she felt like she would be taken under by the insurmountable amount of stress, she was struck with another realization: Not once had she consulted God about this predicament. She hadn't fallen to her knees to cry out to Him for grace and mercy, not only on her behalf but on behalf of King. She'd been too caught up in the whirlwind of it all, as the rape charge had come at them so fast after their nuptials, she never had a moment to truly breathe and regroup.

She figured now was as good a time as any. It was a little after five a.m., right before daybreak. King was sleeping soundly after yet another night of tossing and turning. While the apartment was calm and quiet, Tatum decided to kneel before the sofa in the living room, right as the sun was rising above the horizon from their panoramic windows, which overlooked Central Park.

But once Tatum was in position, she didn't know what to say. A part of her still wondered if King was truly innocent. Would it be fair to ask God to let a guilty man go free? Tatum recalled Gya once saying that whenever someone was experiencing a loss of words on how to pray, just seek God for His will and ask that His will be done, and that's exactly what Tatum did. By the end of her heartfelt prayer, Tatum was a mess of tears, and all she could do was just continue to cry out for God's help. And once she stood up, rubbing at her growing belly, she had a feeling that all would be alright. Of course the prayer hadn't been a magic potion to make everything go away, but Tatum now felt she had the strength to endure whatever else came at her. She felt an assurance that God was at her side every step of the way. He always had been. He was just waiting for her to acknowledge Him. It was also in that moment that Tatum felt sure about King's innocence. King would never have to force his way on any woman. Tatum didn't know what this Whitney hoped to gain from these accusations, although she had a strong suspicion it was a cash come-up, but

Tatum resolved to make it her daily prayer that God would cause the truth to come to light.

***

Ariana's husband, Russell, was officially traded to the Toronto Raptors. Tatum called up her friend to state how much she'd miss her.

"I'm gonna miss you and Kels so much too. I know I'm gonna be a big mess at the going-away party Kelsea is hosting."

"Kels is hosting a party for you guys?" Tatum asked.

Ariana paused. "Uh, yeah. Didn't you know?"

"No. This is the first I'm hearing about it."

"Oh, wow. Well...this is rather awkward."

"Don't worry about it, Ari. Kelsea has been acting shady toward me since the allegations first broke, so I'm not surprised she would exclude me and King."

"While I respect it's her home, she should've left it up to me to decide whether or not I wanted you guys present since the party is being hosted in our honor. Do you want me to talk to her?"

"No, Ari. I'm not going to grovel and beg anyone for an invite to *anything*," Tatum said, her voice full of adamance.

Once hanging up with Ariana, Tatum called her mom, Vanessa, to vent about the hurtfulness of Kelsea's snub.

"Adversity often shows you who your true friends are. Kelsea is the epitome of a fair-weather friend. Once King is cleared of everything, don't allow her to come traipsing back into your life. When a person shows you who they are, believe them," Vanessa advised.

***

"So how are you feeling, now that the divorce paperwork has officially been filed?" Hannah asked Gya as she sat in an armchair in Gya's hotel room.

Gya stood gazing out the window, rubbing her growing belly and taking in the brightness of the Atlanta summer day. It was a stark contrast to the somberness within her heart. Filing the paperwork made the looming divorce all the more real. Gya thought she'd be relieved, but she only felt sadness at the demise of a short-lived marriage. Again, she felt like a failure.

"That's a loaded question, Hannah."

"Trust me, I understand, but there's something I wanted to make you aware of. Word has it that this Mercedes girl is in talks to be casted on a new reality show called *Sidepieces*."

Gya whirled around from the window, nearly making herself dizzy. "What?"

"Yes. I know you're still on the social media sabbatical, which explains why you haven't heard about it, but I didn't want you to be totally blindsided."

"Forgive me, Hannah, but I could kill both her and Bryant right now. I wasn't raised to hate anyone, but why can't she just go away? Now she's trying to profit off making my life miserable. Some women have no shame, and I regret the day I ever crossed paths with her or her treacherous cousin, Christal. I can't believe I once considered Christal to be a friend."

"If this turns out to be true, you need to consult an attorney and file a gag order against her. Mercedes won't be able to mention your name on the show without financial repercussions. For now, try to calm down. I don't want your blood pressure spiking and upsetting the baby. Let's just change the subject. Now I do have some good news. I'm planning a spiritual midwife conference for later this year. You will be done with your ministry sabbatical by then, and if you're feeling up to it, I'd like for you to be one of the conference speakers and share your miscarriage story along with how God restored you to conceive again."

"And how I'm now facing life as a single mother? Do you really think the women present at this conference will find that encouraging?"

"The focal point is believing God for conception. I counsel many women who battle with infertility and multiple miscarriages. I love sharing testimonies that show them there is hope. Can you put your feelings of inadequacy aside and think about uplifting these women who need it?"

Gya nodded. "I'll think about it." But she honestly didn't see how the state of her life could serve to uplift anyone. She could barely uplift herself.

Once Hannah left, Gya phoned Bryant and demanded to know if the rumor about Mercedes being casted on that trashy reality show was valid.

"Yeah, I heard about that too. I actually talked to her, and she said she'd auditioned."

"So you're still in contact with that tr—? You know what, never mind. What you do from here on out is none of my business, but I will be taking out a gag order against her. She'd better keep my name out of her mouth, or I will sue her into oblivion."

"Yeah, I plan to do the same. She won't be able to mention me by name either."

Gya laughed derisively. "She had more than your name in her mouth last year, didn't she? That's why we're in this craziness to begin with. I really can't stand the both of you, Bryant. Thank you for continuing to make my life miserable."

With those final words, Gya hung up in his face.

***

"You're having a baby girl," Dr. Pattison, Tatum's OB/GYN, informed her and King.

King gripped Tatum's hand and gave the first genuine smile she'd seen from him in weeks.

"Dad, are you disappointed? Were you hoping for a boy?" Dr. Pattison kidded.

King kissed Tatum's hand. "I'm ecstatic, doc. I just wanted a healthy child, and I can't wait to hold my little princess this November."

As King and Tatum left the doctor's office hand in hand and prepared to enter into their chauffeured black Town Car, there were two paparazzi stationed outside.

"Did you find out what you were having, King? How did the doctor's visit go? Will you miss your child if you're convicted?"

Both Tatum and King ignored the questions and climbed into the vehicle. Being stalked by the paparazzi was now their new normal, which was why neither King nor Tatum ventured out of the house much. As the car pulled away, Tatum closed her eyes and continued to pray for God's strength to weather the storm.

Chapter Nine

The purity conference in July arrived before Gya realized it, and she had to admit the planning kept her occupied. While in the planning phase, she didn't have time to sit and mope about Bryant, Mercedes, or the demise of her marriage and impending divorce. And the social media detox was working wonders upon her psyche, as she felt a disconnect from the tabloid fodder and other foolishness. She also took a break from watching the local and world news, only tuning in once a week to stay abreast of important current events.

"I can already tell God is going to do a mighty work through this conference because the devil is already busy," Hannah told Gya. "I'm receiving a bit of backlash from some women, citing that our purity conference is placing too much pressure upon young ladies. I'm under fire for not holding young men accountable as well. Of course, there's also some feminist groups proclaiming I'm suppressing sexual liberation. I'm trying my best to just focus on this godly assignment and tune out all the noise."

She also shared with Gya her plans of creating a gospel record label. Hannah had already signed a female gospel trio called The Holy Trinity, which consisted of the lead singer, Trinity, and backup vocalists Dejah and London. The girls were in their early twenties like Gya, and she'd really taken a liking to them. They were very sweet and down to earth.

"They're going to be the gospel version of Destiny's Child. Just watch," Hannah boasted.

The Holy Trinity opened the conference with a medley of songs that set the atmosphere ablaze with praise and worship. All of the young ladies looked beautiful in their white gowns, and Gya teared up seeing her vision come to life even though it was orchestrated through Hannah.

Once each young lady was presented with her purity ring, Hannah did an altar call. Gya joined Hannah at the altar as she prayed over the young women, laying hands upon each of them in prayer as well. Once done, Gya was enveloped in a cacophony of glory. Oh, how she'd missed ministering to young ladies. Once her sabbatical officially ended, she felt she'd be more powerful than ever.

During the luncheon portion of the conference, several of the young ladies Gya prayed for approached her to thank her and tell her that they enjoyed and missed her social media content. They were greatly anticipating her return. It warmed Gya's heart when they shared that they didn't judge her for her failed marriage and still felt the message of purity was important despite her bad outcome. Gya really needed to hear that and couldn't wait to return to her mission.

But not everyone was happy, and Gya found this out later that evening when Hannah came to her hotel room.

"You were totally out of order this afternoon, Gya. Did you not take heed to the warning I gave you from God about trying to minister to others while you are in the healing stage?"

Gya was taken aback by the brusqueness she heard in Hannah's tone.

"Now wait just one minute, Hannah. I don't appreciate your tone. I realize you're older than me, but I am no child, and I will not be spoken to in that manner. And let's not forget this entire conference was my idea in the first place."

"So, you're still hung up on that? I figured that's exactly why you felt it was okay to try and take over today. Honey, it may have been your idea, but *my* money and connections pulled this off, let's get that straight. You are still bitter about the divorce and learning that your husband's mistress is going on that trashy reality show. I can't see how you felt you were in any position to lay hands upon those young ladies. No telling what kind of demonic spirits you've transferred into them."

"Now you're going too far," Gya said, her nostrils flaring in anger.

"No, Gya, you really need to learn humility. Take my chastening of you today as a spirit of tough love and godly correction. As your spiritual mentor, I'm at liberty to do just that. It's what you signed up for when you agreed to come here to Atlanta, all at my expense need I remind you."

"But I didn't sign up to be controlled and domineered by anyone."

Hannah smirked. "*Hmmph.* Perhaps that's another reason your marriage didn't work out then." With those last words, Hannah grabbed her purse and sashayed out of the hotel suite, leaving a dumbfounded and furious Gya to stare after her.

Gya was so upset that she couldn't sleep. She didn't understand where Hannah got off talking to her like that, and then had the nerve to throw her failed marriage in her face when she knew that was a sore spot for Gya. She'd lost a lot of respect for Hannah. But if Gya was honest with herself, the writing was on the wall when she'd had dinner at Hannah's home, seeing her unruly kids and how she took advantage of the nanny. Not to mention the stolen purity conference idea. And now this ungodly spiritual rebuke.

When Gya awakened after a restless night of sleep, she sent Hannah a text informing her she was cutting her stay in Atlanta short and ending the mentorship, effective immediately. Hannah phoned soon thereafter.

"Aren't you tired of fleeing, Gya? You're just like Jonah within the Bible. You fled from Miami when you learned of your husband's infidelity, and now you're ready to flee from Atlanta because you're mad at me. You're not in college anymore, Gya. You're an adult, and adults talk rationally and discuss issues. You can't keep running from every problem you face."

"You didn't speak to me rationally last night, Hannah."

"You're right, Gya, and for that, I apologize. And honestly before you texted me, I was going to call and apologize because I know the Holy Spirit is not pleased with how I handled things last night. I don't want any smoke with God about how I care for his flock. I was out of line with how I spoke to you. I sincerely apologize."

Gya knew as a Christian she was obligated to accept Hannah's apology and extend grace, but she was still pretty angry.

"Now I can't stop you from leaving, but I encourage you to finish out your remaining time here in Atlanta. Just like Jonah, God has you here on assignment. If you choose not to stay, that's on you."

Gya wanted to do just that, but it was bothering her that Hannah accused her of always running from her problems. She wasn't the type to ever back down, so she decided to be her usual stubborn self and tough things out, if only to prove a point that she was no coward.

Gya sighed and told Hannah she accepted her apology and was willing to stay and honor her commitment to remain in Atlanta for the duration of the summer. But she definitely wasn't as fond of Hannah anymore and no longer trusted her.

Chapter Ten

Tatum felt it was time to regain control of her life. After all, she wasn't the one on trial. Often when she was bored, she'd watch makeup tutorials on YouTube and then practice on her own face. She felt confident enough to start her own YouTube channel with makeup tutorials along with inspirational messages to viewers as she worked. Her first video was a smash hit with over a million views. Tatum figured a lot of people tuned in to be nosey, thinking she would drop some tea about the trial or the future of her marriage with King. But due to the gag order, she couldn't talk about the trial, and the state of her marriage was no one's business. Of course, Tatum had to delete and block a lot of nasty comments, which she'd expected and braced herself for.

Tatum found her new hobby rather therapeutic and began to upload videos weekly. She also became more active on TikTok, garnering thousands of followers on the popular and trending platform.

Tatum was tired of being lukewarm with God. When she would encounter storms within her life, she sought Him out but would taper off on her prayer time and worship once the storms cleared. But God had been so gracious and patient with her. This time around, Tatum wanted to be all in and show the world that she sought comfort and solace through the Father as she dealt with this present fiasco with King.

***

"I can't believe how much my YouTube channel has grown, Gya, and I'm almost addicted to TikTok. It's such a fun platform. But I'm careful not to make this into an idol," Tatum shared with Gya over the phone, her voice full of excitement.

"Please don't, cousin. You see exactly how that worked out for me. I'm glad you're finding your niche."

"Yes, it's definitely a great distraction from all of this madness with King."

"I'm proud of you, cousin. I wish I could tune in to your videos weekly, but I'm still on my social media hiatus and detox. It was actually Hannah who told me about your content. It's managed to capture her attention as well."

"How are things in Atlanta?" Tatum asked. "I know you've been off social media, but has Hannah mentioned anything about the allegations being brought against her?"

Gya frowned. "What allegations?"

"You know how Hannah conducts those spiritual midwife conferences in different cities each year? Well, several women have come forward blasting her on social media and citing that the conferences are nothing but a scam. Hannah has been getting these women to sow into her ministry according to the number of children they desire for God to bless them with. For example, if a woman wants two children then sow two hundred dollars into her ministry and watch how God will move on their behalf. If they want four children, then sow four hundred dollars, and so on."

"Are you serious, Tay?" Gya was disgusted but not really surprised. "And no, Hannah hasn't mentioned a word about it. And to think she invited me to be a speaker for the conference she's conducting this fall." Gya hesitated and then spilled about all that had occurred between her and Hannah since she arrived in Atlanta and how she'd become turned off by Hannah's character.

"Perhaps God wanted you to see what Hannah was really like so you could stop placing her on a pedestal. I know it's disappointing. Hey, do you want me to put you in contact with the PI I hired to trail King? I bet she can find some skeletons Hannah is hiding in her closet. From what you shared with me about her attitude and behavior, I think it's time for the façade to be taken down."

"Yeah, you can give me her info, but I'm not too comfortable with bringing down another sister. I'll leave the exposing to God. It seems like He's already at work with these women who've come forward. I hate that Hannah took advantage of their vulnerability for motherhood. Perhaps I should just pack my stuff and leave."

"I honestly think you should stay a bit longer and uncover the truth about her. It's easier to get any info you need while you're there in Atlanta, right there in her camp. Use this time to your advantage. And you should strongly consider reaching out to the PI," Tatum advised.

Once Gya hung up, she reflected on Tatum's words about getting more info on Hannah. Gya was curious as to what the PI would uncover. She decided she would reach out to this woman and see if it would be discovered that Hannah was nothing but another wolf in sheep's clothing as Gya suspected.

Chapter Eleven

"She changed her mind and wants to settle," King said to Tatum. "Daniel just called me."

Tatum stared at King incredulously. She also noted how whenever they discussed the case he never mentioned his accuser, Whitney Prescott, by name. "Wait a minute. What kind of mess is this? If she's adamant that you raped her, wouldn't she want to see you prosecuted?"

"She's citing that this case has taken a toll on her mental health, and she feels going to trial will only worsen things for her emotionally. Her attorney is ready to tell the prosecution team she doesn't want to move forward with a trial and will refuse to testify," King explained.

"How can the prosecution not see that her allegations were only a ploy for cash? To me, it's now pretty obvious she fabricated being raped. So are you going to settle? You don't want to try and fight this in court?"

"I'm torn, Tatum. I realize that by agreeing to the settlement it's like I'm admitting to being guilty, but I mean it: I did not rape that girl. But, on the other hand, I just want all of this to go away. I'm afraid of the risk of going to trial. What if I'm convicted? It's like I've said from the very beginning, I feel the court will try to make an example out of me. It's a lose-lose situation all around. What do you think I should do?"

Tatum raised her hands in a gesture of absolving herself of any responsibility. "I can't make this decision for you, King, but I'll support whatever you decide."

"And that's why I love you," King said, coming over to kiss her and rub her protruding belly. He released a long sigh. "I'm going to settle. No matter what this may cause the public to think about me, I want to be there for you and our daughter. I can't do that behind bars."

Tatum nodded in agreement. "You do what you feel is best, King."

***

When the news broke of King's settlement with his accuser, it set the news media ablaze. The general public was divided once again with half feeling the settlement was an admission of guilt on King's part. This was further compounded by the statement he released in which he actually apologized to his accuser for making her feel threatened during their sexual encounter. Tatum wondered if King would ever fully bounce back from this debacle as he was being crucified in the press once again, sealing his fall from grace as the beloved emerging sports darling of New York City.

Chapter Twelve

"Erinn, what do you think about those women who've come forward about Hannah?" Gya casually asked Hannah's nanny one Sunday after church as they prepared to leave after service. Gya had already contacted the PI and started the probe into Hannah's background, but she figured it couldn't hurt to squeeze some tea out of Erinn.

"Simply preposterous. They are acting as if Hannah is God. All she can do is pray over your womb, but if you don't conceive then she can't be blamed for that," Erinn said.

Gya knew she was probably pushing her limits, as Erinn was devoutly loyal to Hannah, but she decided to go for it. "Didn't you say the former nanny slandered Hannah and her family too? What was her name? Is she among those women who've come forward?"

"Her name is Alexis—Alexis Moore. And I wouldn't be surprised if she was behind all this in an attempt to get back at Hannah. She and her husband fled to Tulsa, Oklahoma, after leaving this church. No telling what kind of havoc they are wreaking there," Erinn said. "But we need to stop talking about this because Hannah wouldn't want us gossiping within the church, much less about her."

"You're absolutely right, Erinn. Please forgive me, and excuse my manners," Gya said, playing into Erinn's naiveté.

The PI emailed Gya with her report within a week, and what was uncovered was absolutely astounding. Hannah's birth name was Kaylin Lee, and it turned out her mother was not deceased as she'd shared with Gya when she'd first come to Atlanta. Her mother was listed as a Dorinda Powell, and she resided in Baltimore. Kaylin/Hannah was the eldest of two children. She had a younger sister who was incarcerated and serving a life term for her role in an armed robbery that resulted in the death of a convenience store clerk.

"Hannah is nothing but a pathological liar," Gya muttered under her breath as she continued to read the report on Shawn, learning he was engaged to a woman by the name of Brandi Carter shortly after graduating from Morgan State. She wondered if this was the "Peninnah" whom Hannah referenced during her testimony. Breaking her social media hiatus, Gya got online and did some digging. Through looking at old photos from The Living Word's Facebook page, she saw pics of Hannah and Alexis Moore together. She then searched for Alexis' personal Facebook profile. Gya was straightforward in her inbox message to Alexis, stating that she was having suspicions about Hannah. She also mentioned being aware that Alexis had signed an NDA, but she wanted to have a private and confidential conversation with her concerning Hannah's character. Gya then searched for Brandi Carter and messaged her as well, telling her she wanted some information about Kaylin.

Brandi responded within an hour, providing her number, and Gya phoned her immediately.

"I haven't heard the name Kaylin in years, so I knew you were pretty legit if you were referring to Hannah by that name. I simply despise that woman. She's nothing but a snake."

"She told me you resent her because Shawn chose her over you," Gya probed.

"No. Shawn was *my* boyfriend first. Kaylin and I were college roommates at Morgan State, and she was one of my best friends. After bringing Kaylin home to meet my parents during our freshman year, my mom shared that she sensed Kaylin was jealous of me, but I didn't listen. Kaylin grew up with a mother who was on drugs, and her younger sister followed in her mom's wayward footsteps and embarked on a life of crime. She was always ashamed of her family background. I was proud of Kaylin for attending college on a scholarship and trying to make something of herself, but she turned out to be nothing but a treacherous snake. Once we graduated, she and I actually lost contact, but I didn't know her distance was due to the fact that she and Shawn slept together behind my back a few months after our graduation. The next thing I know, she's showing up at Shawn's doorstep with toddler twin boys and telling him that he's the father. He and I had just gotten engaged, but I called things off immediately once Kaylin came to me and confessed everything, admitting she'd distanced herself from me out of guilt and trying to hide her pregnancy."

"Wait. What? She said she gave birth to the twins after she and Shawn got married after having multiple miscarriages."

"Nothing but lies. It came to light that she was never even pregnant because she has no uterus. She underwent an emergency hysterectomy while in her teens due to some injury and had to have her uterus removed. Those twins she tried to pass off as Shawn's actually belong to her sister. She was pregnant when she was convicted and sentenced, giving birth to them in prison. Kaylin got custody of the boys and then tried to lie and tell Shawn he was their father. She's no different from her mom or her sister if you ask me because she's now robbing people in the name of God."

Gya was floored by all that Brandi was sharing. "So Shawn knows the twins aren't his?"

"Yes. He immediately had a blood test done and found out Kaylin lied, and he found out about her hysterectomy after a conversation with her mom, but since I wouldn't take him back I believe he just settled and stayed with her. I guess a part of him felt sorry for her."

Gya couldn't understand how Shawn could marry a person like Hannah who was capable of so many lies, and then to actually form a ministry with her. Gya was beyond disgusted with them both.

"So that means Reagan is adopted too."

"Yes, she is, but I have no clue about how she came into their lives. I kicked both Shawn and Kaylin completely to the curb after their betrayal and never looked back. I'm now happily married with two children of my own."

Once Gya hung up with Brandi, her mind was still reeling at the details of Hannah's double life. She pretended her mom was dead because she was ashamed of her family background and then took her sister's twin boys and embarked on a life of lies with Shawn in compliance? It was so absurd.

Alexis Moore finally responded to Gya's Facebook inbox message the following day.

"I'll admit I was hesitant to respond to you. I wondered if Hannah had put you up to contacting me and was trying to lure me into some trap."

Gya assured her that she came with no ill intent and just wanted further insight on how Hannah was using and manipulating other women. She revealed how Erinn was being used by Hannah, and Alexis merely laughed.

"Not surprising to hear. Erinn has been up Hannah's behind since she first joined The Living Word, and she was always jealous of our close relationship. I truly considered Hannah a good friend, which is why I was comfortable with becoming her nanny. I'm sure Erinn gladly filled my shoes once my husband and I left Atlanta. My husband was the church accountant, and he discovered that both Hannah and Shawn were misusing church funds. When my husband began to ask too many questions, they turned on us and accused us of being Judases and trying to take them down. They would take subliminal digs at us during Sunday sermons and on social media. I finally had enough of the bullying and intimidation and decided to leave. I felt it was an answered prayer from God when my husband found a position with a reputable accounting firm in Tulsa. Caring for Hannah's children was nothing but a headache, but being aware of her past infertility woes and how much she treasured them, I tried to be empathetic."

Gya informed Alexis that the infertility and miscarriage stories were nothing but a fabrication, and all of her children were adopted.

Alexis paused. "Wow. To my understanding, only Reagan was adopted. Hannah once revealed to me that the twins actually belonged to Shawn and were conceived from an affair he'd had early in their marriage. She decided to forgive him and raise the boys as her own since she was having such a hard time conceiving."

Gya couldn't help but laugh. It was yet another lie Hannah had concocted, and Gya filled Alexis in on all that she'd discovered through her private investigation.

"Wow. So those boys are really her nephews? You know I wasn't going to say anything, but I've heard murmurings over the years that Reagan belonged to a woman at their former church in Baltimore—a church she and Shawn used to attend before moving to Atlanta and launching The Living Word. The woman ended up dying in childbirth, and they assumed custody of Reagan. I heard they paid off Reagan's grandmother to allow them to have full custody and even had a fake document produced that stated Reagan's birth mother appointed Hannah as legal guardian, should anything ever happen to her. I brushed it off as a wild and audacious rumor at the time, but given all you've shared, the story is not too implausible."

Gya's mind was spinning crazily with each new development.

"All of these women who've come forward about Hannah aren't lying because I was foolish enough to fall for the same thing when I was trying to conceive my first child. I sowed money into Hannah and The Living Word faithfully, thinking that in turn, God would honor my faithfulness and bless me with a child. He did, but not because of my sowing. It was because He is *God*. I hope many other women see the light before being blinded by Hannah and her conniving ways. She's nothing but a lying manipulator. I'm not surprised she's latched on to you because she's always wanted to reach the younger demographic. I know her taking you under her wing was nothing but her trying to use you in order to gain access to your platform."

Gya thanked Alexis for her time and assured her that everything shared through their phone call would remain confidential.

***

After all she'd uncovered about Hannah's past, Gya decided it was time to leave Atlanta, but she wanted to be a woman of integrity and honor her commitment to assist with The Living Word's women's brunch as she'd promised. The brunch was held the following Saturday afternoon at the Atlanta Evergreen Lakeside resort. The food and fellowship portion had just gotten underway when one of the ladies present mentioned to Gya how blessed she was by Tatum's videos. Hannah was within earshot and laughed in derision.

"Tatum is yet another fly-by-night pseudo minister, and I'm tired of all of these women who lack true anointing trying to establish platforms on social media. Without God's full grace, their ministries won't last."

Gya's eyes blazed with anger, and she released a long sigh that rivaled a rusty hinge. She was highly offended at Hannah's scathing words about her cousin. But as Gya thought about it, she couldn't ever recall Hannah having anything good to say about other women in ministry. Hannah didn't have any female friends outside of the women in her church congregation who worshipped the ground she walked on. Gya realized it was insecurity on Hannah's part, and she masked the insecurity by trying to come off as if she were better than other women, and no one was holier and more anointed than her.

"Excuse me, ladies. I'll be leaving now."

A hushed silence fell over the room as Gya grabbed her purse and exited.

She had just reached the entrance of the resort when she heard Hannah call out to her.

"I'm leaving Atlanta," Gya said firmly as she watched Hannah approach, "and I *won't* be talked into staying this time."

"That's just as well because I was going to ask you to leave anyhow. I'm also rescinding the offer I extended to you to be a speaker at my upcoming conference this fall. I know you've been trying to get dirt on me from Erinn. I don't need any sneaky gossips in my camp," Hannah said, her voice dripping with venomous anger.

Gya wasn't surprised Erinn had revealed her probing to Hannah, as she'd expected as much from the blind follower.

"As a matter of fact, I'm inclined to sue you for all expenses I incurred to cover your stay here in Atlanta. Oh, how I regret it all," Hannah continued.

"Keep in mind that *you* sought me out and brought me here. I didn't ask you for one cent, but just to show you that money is of no consequence to me, I'm willing to reimburse you for each and every dime. I don't want to be indebted to you for any reason."

"Of course, money is of no consequence to you," Hannah scoffed. "You only have it because of Bryant, and I'm quite sure the divorce settlement will leave you sitting pretty. It's so unfair to women like me who've had to work hard and struggle for everything we have."

"Yeah, I know all about the struggle you went through to adopt your three children, *Kaylin,*" Gya spat. She then took immense pleasure at the look of shock that fell across Hannah's face at the mention of her birth name. "Yes, you heard me right. I'm privy to your fabricated pregnancy stories and how your entire ministry is built on a bunch of lies. And I want no part of it or *you* anymore for that matter."

After dropping that final bombshell, Gya stalked outside and whipped out her cell phone to order an Uber. As she waited for the rideshare to take her back to the hotel to pack her things, Gya let out an exhale of relief that she'd finally knocked Hannah off her high horse.

Chapter Thirteen

In September, the NFL season was in full swing, and the NBA preseason was also underway. Tatum was excluded from watch parties at Kelsea's home this season, although she and Kelsea still followed each other on Instagram and TikTok. Now that Ariana had moved to Canada, and Tatum was no longer in the picture, Kelsea had befriended the girlfriend of a recently traded player to the New York City Flash. Tatum saw photos of Kelsea and the girl hanging out via IG, and they recorded fun and silly TikTok reels together. Kelsea was the only close friend Tatum made in New York City, and she felt the void of her desertion. She'd made one last attempt to extend an olive branch to Kelsea, but it was a stilted phone conversation full of awkward pauses. Finally, Kelsea came right out and told Tatum that she couldn't support her staying married to a rapist.

"I know Antoine has not been a saint for the duration of our marriage, but he's never been accused of anything of this magnitude."

"Would you leave him if he had?" Tatum pressed.

"Look, Tatum, I don't have time for this. This is not the time for hypotheticals."

"The fact that you can't give me a straight answer confirms to me that you don't know what you'd do if Antoine was in that same situation, so how can you act so high and mighty and judge me and King?"

"I'm hanging up now. Besides, with your new massive social media following, you no longer need my friendship. Goodbye, Tatum." With those last words, Kelsea hung up, officially solidifying the end of their friendship.

The only person Tatum could grieve the loss of her friend with was her mother, Vanessa.

"Trust me, Tatum, you'll see that you're better off without her in your life. And it sounds like she's jealous of your newfound social media fame. She's nothing but a housewife who lives in Antoine's shadow while you're carving out your own identity outside of King. Screw her and Antoine's soon-to-be washed-up behind," Vanessa said.

Tatum felt Gya could relate to the betrayal of a friend, as the reality show *Sidepieces* aired in mid-September. Tatum watched as Mercedes came on screen and boasted about how she'd first crossed paths with Bryant at Gya's birthday party, which she attended with her cousin Christal who was once a friend of Gya's. Of course, due to the gag order both Gya and Bryant enforced, she couldn't mention either by name. She then detailed how Christal's husband, Victor, Bryant's fellow teammate, snuck her into their training camp and brought her to Bryant's room.

"We were just sitting on the bed talking, making casual conversation, and that's when I made my move," Mercedes said. Despite a few lingering post-pregnancy pounds, Tatum had to admit that Mercedes was an attractive woman. She exuded sex appeal as opposed to Gya's girl-next-door beauty. Tatum figured this was what drew Bryant in, yet she was disgusted at Mercedes' boldness in describing her seduction of him to the world.

Christal even made an appearance on the show. There was a scene where she and Mercedes were dining in a restaurant and chatting. Mercedes admitted that Bryant had been an active father in their newborn's life.

"I know the wifey has started divorce proceedings, and I'm hoping he'll consider making us official. I'd love to get a commitment from him so the three of us can be a happy family. I'd love to give him more children," Mercedes said.

Tatum couldn't help but roll her eyes at this girl's delusion.

"Have you crossed paths with wifey?" Christal asked.

"No. I heard she relocated to Atlanta, which is not very far from Miami. I feel like she's trying to be closer to him. I hope it's just for the sake of their child and not because she hopes to reconcile. What about you? Have you spoken to her?"

Christal tossed her head back and laughed. "Girl, you know I'm the last person she'd want to talk to. She totally hates my guts, and you know I'd tell you if I had."

Tatum had seen enough and changed the channel. She regretted even tuning in for a peek of that foolishness. She felt so bad for Gya. She couldn't imagine Whitney Prescott signing up to be on a reality show and gloating about her sexual relations with King.

Tatum's phone rang, and she saw it was Gya.

"Hey, cousin. What's up?"

"Are you watching *Sidepieces*?" Gya asked.

"Yeah, I couldn't help myself. I tuned in for a bit before turning it off in disgust."

"It's like I'm a glutton for punishment 'cause I watched out of curiosity as well. I'll admit I'm hurt by their cavalier attitudes toward my pain. I mean, granted Mercedes doesn't owe me anything, but I thought Christal was a friend."

"Karma will have the last say for both of them. I know exactly what you're going through because Kelsea has told me in no uncertain terms that she doesn't want to continue our friendship, and I respect her decision."

"How is King faring during the preseason?"

"He feels like a social outcast. Things were tense when he first came to New York City due to his cockiness and arrogance, but now he feels frozen out on a different level. Not just by his teammates, but fans as well. He's booed during the player intros at every home game and in each city the Flash travels to. It breaks my heart to see him hurting and crushed under public judgment."

"You just have to continue to pray and trust God. But can I be honest? Given my experience with Hannah, I've become very disenchanted with the church. I never thought I'd be the one to say something of that nature, but it seems like every time you look at social media, there's a story of yet another Christian leader caught up in some foolishness. Not everyone deserves a platform."

"You have to remember though, Gya, people are human. And think of the many biblical heroes that fell out of grace with God."

"Yeah but I just feel if you accept the call to be God's representative on a large public platform then you're held to a higher standard. That's what so frustrating about my divorce from Bryant. I honored my marriage vows, but my ministry platform was cast in a bad light due to *his* transgressions."

"Maybe you should've married a pastor," Tatum joked.

"That's another gamble as well 'cause, like I said, a lot of those jokers get caught up too. Let me get off this phone. This conversation has grown depressing, and I'm doing everything to safeguard Landon from negative emotions."

"Continue to hang in there, cousin. Love you. I can't wait to hold and spoil my new baby cousin soon."

"Oh goodness. Between you and my parents, Landon is going to be rotten." Gya laughed.

Chapter Fourteen

What was being dubbed as the Hannah Heals Spiritual Abuse scandal continued to heat up, and God was continuing to pull the blinders off through The Holy Trinity, the group Hannah signed to her record label. The trio of young ladies were guests on *The Lauryn Roberts Show*. Lauryn was a YouTube gospel tabloid commentator who brought exposure to false prophets and fallen church leaders. Hannah's record label seemed to fold before it could officially launch, and the trio's deal with Hannah soured, leaving them out of thousands of dollars.

"Hannah made us pay out of pocket for our own studio time, and we also paid for a lot of our marketing and promotion. Each of us charged these expenses on credit cards, which leaves us drowning in debt. We now realize these expenses should've been handled by Hannah and the label. She totally conned us," Trinity said to Lauryn with eyes full of tears.

"So what's next for the group?" Lauryn asked.

"We aren't giving up, and it's our prayer to be signed to a more reputable label. We also plan to sue Hannah for the debt we incurred." Her two bandmates, Dejah and London, nodded in agreement.

Gya's heart went out to the young ladies. Hannah seemed to prey on the young and naïve, and she was glad the house of cards Hannah built appeared to be crumbling.

Meanwhile, with football season officially underway, the Miami Waves were off to a strong start, driven in part by Bryant who was starting his sophomore season with great numbers and stats. Gya learned this from her father who still supported Bryant, but she couldn't bring herself to watch any of the games. She was now mere weeks away from giving birth, and she didn't want to transition into childbirth stressed on any level. Not by Hannah, Bryant, or anyone else.

In what Gya felt was an act of duplicity, Lauryn announced that Hannah would be a guest on her show, after trashing her. She stated she wanted to give Hannah an opportunity to defend her name, but Gya felt it was only a ploy for ratings and a popularity boost for the show. The ploy seemed to work because over thirty thousand people tuned in for the live-stream interview, and against her better judgment, Gya was among them.

Hannah looked very haggard, as the social media firestorm around her character seemed to be taking its toll on her appearance. She had dark circles under her eyes and consistently dabbed at them with a tissue as Lauryn introduced her and welcomed her onto the show. She then dived right in and pulled no punches.

"So, Hannah, tell the masses truthfully, did you misuse your prophetic gifting and take advantage of women?"

"First off, let me say no. It has never been my intent to misuse anyone. I understand when you are called to a high office the enemy is always lurking in the shadows, looking to take you down, and he's doing it through people I once tried to help, which makes it all the more hurtful."

"Well, to give my two cents, I believe a lot of people treat you social media ministers like semi-gods. They act like needy, lost sheep clamoring for your time and attention, and this is how they set themselves up to be hurt and disappointed when you don't meet their expectations," Lauryn said, doing her trademark sip from the cup of tea she kept on hand for each show.

"Lauryn, I beg to differ, as I'm not just a social media minister. I own and operate a highly anointed church alongside my gifted husband, Shawn, and I have never been the type to want people to place me on a high pedestal."

Yeah, right, Gya thought with a roll of her eyes.

"As a matter of fact, I think this controversy I find myself in is all at the hands of the last young lady I tried to help and mentor. We're all familiar with Gya Green and her fall out of favor when she was caught up in her own scandal with her philandering husband. Now *she* fits your description of a social media minister. She was nothing but trouble from the very beginning of me graciously flying her out to Atlanta and hosting her at my full expense," Hannah said and then proceeded to detail how Gya took over the altar call during the purity conference that past summer.

Gya's eyes ballooned at Hannah's gall.

"I sensed in my spirit that Gya was jealous of my platform because it's a level she strived to obtain before her husband's infidelity ran her off social media in shame. I'll admit her actions were very hurtful because I reached out to her in a place of love and tried to nurse her broken heart to a healed place. She was even considering a late-term abortion of her child to get back at her husband, which I talked her out of."

Gya almost lost total control of her bladder. She couldn't believe Hannah would reveal something so confidential. She was beyond stunned.

"And I also considered alerting the authorities because she threatened the life of her husband's mistress once she learned she would be appearing on that sleazy new reality show called *Sidepieces*."

Gya's mouth dropped.

"She actually told you she would kill her?" Lauryn pressed.

"I've said too much as it is. I don't want to discuss that any further," Hannah said.

Gya had seen enough. She yelled out for her mom, and she heard the urgency in Pam's footsteps as she came up the stairs and practically flew inside of Gya's bedroom.

"Gya, what is it? Did your water break?"

"No. Hannah is slandering me on *The Lauryn Roberts Show*."

"Gya, why are you even tuned in to that foolishness?"

"I'm going to sue her for defamation."

"Gya, she is not worth it. Your main focus should be giving birth in a few weeks. The enemy is just using all this as a distraction. There is nothing more joyous than being a mother for the first time."

"Mom, that joy left when I left Bryant. Don't you see that? I'm not happy about this pregnancy. There, I said it. I'm not happy about this pregnancy," Gya repeated, breaking down in tears. Hannah revealing her secret desire for an abortion reinforced that she was faking the funk when it came to her pregnancy. Gya realized she was more scared than ever at the prospect of being a single mother. Now she feared she would have to deal with postpartum depression heaped upon her doubts about being an effective mother.

Pam came and sat next to her on the bed, consoling her. "Gya, your feelings are normal. Those pregnancy hormones are well at work, and I understand you're scared, but your father and I will be with you every step of the way. We'll help you love and raise Landon. You have nothing to worry about. He will be well taken care of. And as much as you hate to accept this, I know Bryant loves him just as much. I believe the two of you can effectively co-parent. You are not in this alone."

"I don't understand how someone like Hannah can have such a strong prophetic gifting yet be so evil."

"Romans eleven and twenty-nine states that gifts come without repentance. She's operating through God's grace, but if she continues to do evil, trust me, His anointing will depart from her. God is not mocked."

"I am so turned off from organized religion right now. I don't know if I'll ever step foot in a church again. You don't know which shepherds are trustworthy anymore."

"Stop talking foolish. Landon will be raised within the knowledge of God. I don't play when it comes to children being brought up in the house of the Lord."

"I never said I stopped believing in God, Mom. I just don't want to be within the church with so many malicious people."

"Gya, the church is full of broken people. It's a hospital for the hurting, so of course you're going to come into contact with flawed people."

"But not the shepherds, Mom. If you accept the calling to lead, to me there's slight margin for error. That's just the way I feel."

"Look, do you need a melatonin? Why don't you relax and try to get some rest?" Pam advised.

Once Pam left the room, Gya felt firm in her resolve to take a lengthy sabbatical from church. Hannah's actions had wounded her heart beyond repair, and she was turned off from ministry. She was spiritually depleted and drained.

Chapter Fifteen

In mid-October, Gya's labor had to be induced since Baby Landon was two weeks past his due date, as he was scheduled to make his debut the first week of October.

"Stubborn little fellow just like his mom and grandpa," Gya's father joked.

The scheduled induction gave Bryant the opportunity to fly in and be present for the birth of his first son. Gya didn't want a C-section, as she'd heard horror stories about the discomfort of the healing process. She was able to have an epidural, and Landon Alexander Green came screaming into the world on the afternoon of October nineteenth. With tears in his eyes, Bryant cut the umbilical cord, and both he and Gya looked on as their son was cleaned up by a nurse and swaddled in a blanket.

Gya held her son close to her bosom and kissed his cheek before passing him over to her parents to love on.

"Thank you for calling me and allowing me to be present to witness the birth of my son, Gya," Bryant said later that evening when they were alone. He had just finished feeding Landon. "I hate to fly back to Miami and leave him behind. Man, this is so tough. I wish I could spend every waking moment with him."

Gya didn't even have a sharp retort, as she was still a bit exhausted from the labor. She merely nodded.

"I hope you'll continue to be fair and allow me to see and spend time with him," Bryant went on.

Again, Gya nodded.

"Gya, are you okay?"

"I'm fine, Bryant. Just tired."

"Understandable. As hard as it is to tear myself away, I'll leave and let you and my little man get some rest. I'll be back in Houston next week to spend some more time with him." Bryant placed Landon inside of his bed at Gya's bedside and then in a surprising move, he placed a soft, tender kiss upon her forehead. Gya closed her eyes at the sensation of his lips upon her skin. It had been so long that the feel of his lips felt almost foreign. But Gya didn't recoil or pull away. Not even when he caressed the side of her face. With a final wink, he left the hospital room.

Gya glanced over at her sleeping newborn and then quickly looked away, thinking about Bryant's question of if she was okay. She would never reveal to Bryant that the answer was no. It would only cause him concern and to probe further. There was no way she could tell Bryant or anyone else that she felt a disconnect from her new son. She went through the motions of kissing and hugging him, but she didn't feel...motherly, and it nearly brought her to tears.

***

True to his word, Bryant was back in Houston the next week to visit Landon. Tatum had flown in earlier in the week to meet her new cousin as well. To Pam's concern, Gya had closed herself off from Landon, and most of his care fell on Pam and Gya's father. None of this was shared with Bryant because Gya feared he would try to pull some crazy move such as filing for full custody.

Bryant was having a great season so far, emerging as one of the Waves' top players. He'd regrouped and conditioned well during the off-season and came back strong in his role as starting running back for the Waves offense. Gya couldn't help but bitterly think about how both Bryant and even Mercedes seemed to be getting ahead these days while she was still scrambling to make sense of her life. It didn't seem fair at all. During her visit, Tatum informed Gya that she'd read a story about how Mercedes hired a security team, citing she was in fear for her life after Hannah revealed that Gya wished her dead. She'd even threatened to file a restraining order against Gya.

It was after Bryant's visit that Pam came into the room and told Gya she needed to get on some type of medication for her postpartum depression and seek counseling.

Gya laughed. "Counseling? You see how seeing a counselor worked out for my marriage? And Hannah was supposed to be my spiritual counselor. How did that work out for me? No, Mom, with all due respect, I'm good on seeking outside sources for help."

"Well, you need to do something because wallowing around here feeling sorry for yourself is not it. I suggest you try and get yourself together. Landon needs you." Pam snapped, and Gya could tell from the firmness within her mother's voice that she was fed up.

"Fine. I'll call the doctor tomorrow and get on an antidepressant," Gya said

"I'm giving you a month to get yourself together, Gya. You're a mother now, and there are no more excuses for you not bonding with your child. I mean it."

Gya made sure her back was turned to her mother before rolling her eyes. She wished she could move away and just leave everyone behind—Bryant, her parents, and even Landon.

Chapter Sixteen

With her own due date drawing near, Tatum was at home in late October watching the Flash play in Boston against the Boston Terriers. As was the norm, King was being booed as he was at the free-throw line. But it wasn't due to the fact that he played for the opposing team. King's reputation was still being slaughtered because of the rape debacle. He ended up missing his first shot, which caused the boos to turn into an eruption of applause from the stands. The crowd then began chanting the word *rapist*. King had just taken his position for his second free-throw attempt when Tatum noticed a cup of liquid come flying from the stands. The cup connected with King's temple, splattering upon his handsome features.

Tatum looked on in disbelief as King went barreling into the stands and accosted who she assumed was the culprit who threw the drink. Tatum was stunned even further as King begin to pummel the guy with his fists. The camera zoomed in on King as he heaped blow upon angry blow and the gentleman tried kicking his legs at King in an attempt to ward him off and defend himself. The crowd was in a frenzy and many of King's teammates ran into the stands to intervene. As Tatum continued to look on, she saw many of the Boston Terrier players clear the bench to join in the fracas, but they only began to wrestle with King and his teammates, further adding fuel to a flame of fury that had now erupted into a full explosion. This was all the incentive the Boston Terrier fans seemed to need to start attacking the Flash players. The feud surged out onto the court and became an all-out free-for-all.

Tatum's forehead began to pound with tension, her features a mask of worry and concern. Her eyebrows furrowed in anguish as she watched the melee. "Oh, this is bad," she muttered, but her words were an understatement.

The sports commentators tried to keep up with the action on the court, their voices resonating with a mixture of excitement and disbelief at the brawl taking place on live television before the eyes of many across the world. Wesley Johnson, a former Flash player who had been traded to Boston that past summer, ran at King and threw a punch to his jaw. King returned the blow with a punch to Wesley's chin, and the two began to go at it as if they were in the middle of a Saturday night main event boxing match in Vegas.

This came as no surprise to Tatum since Wesley and King were archrivals, even when they were teammates. Wesley was extremely jealous of King's popularity when he'd first come to the Flash. They'd had minor scuffles during practice, but tonight their simmering tension seemed to come to a head in Wesley's new stomping grounds of Boston.

The television screen was a mass of fans, players, team personnel, and security trying to bring peace and order. The scene was almost like a riot. Tatum wasn't at all surprised to see uniformed Boston police make their way onto the court and finally bring the brawl to an end. They escorted King and his teammates off the court. Unruly fans who were still within the stands threw beer, popcorn, and a medley of other items at them as they were ushered toward the locker room area amid the sound of raucous boos. The boos grew louder as the police shepherded Boston Terrier players off the court as well. The sports commentator announced he'd just received word that the game would be forfeited and not continue.

Tatum knew a slew of arrests would follow and figured Boston police didn't want to create further controversy by handcuffing African-American players live on national television, especially in a city with a predominantly white population. Not only would King be arrested, but Tatum had no doubt he'd face astronomical fines and a suspension by the league for a few games. What had King been thinking? But Tatum realized he'd reached his breaking point. The stress of the taunts by the fans had been too much, and he'd had enough. But she wished he'd kept his cool. He was now in hot water once again, and she didn't feel his already tarnished reputation could sustain another hit.

Tatum rubbed her belly, as she could feel their daughter actively moving around. *Please don't let me go into early labor behind this madness,* she silently prayed.

***

The Boston Brawl, as it had now infamously been dubbed, dominated the news media for days on end. King and all other players and fans involved in the spectacle had been arrested and faced thousands of dollars in fines. The fan King attacked for throwing the cup of beer at him filed an assault charge against

King, even though he himself had been banned from ever attending another NBA game due to his actions inciting the brawl.

Gya pulled herself out of her funk long enough to call and check on Tatum and to see how King was faring in the midst of yet another controversy.

"It's worse than I thought, Gya. There are talks that the NBA commissioner could ban King from the league altogether. I mean, I was expecting a suspension, but nothing as severe as a ban."

"Even I feel that's a bit extreme. Granted, King was wrong for barreling into the stands like a maniac, but the fan who threw the beer was wrong too. It was totally disrespectful to King. I wished he'd have let law enforcement handle the guy. He would've been escorted out of the arena and fined for assault. Now he has just as strong of a case against King. This is a colossal mess."

"Tell me about it," Tatum sighed.

Gya told her cousin she loved her and that she was in her prayers, but the last statement was one of default. Praying was the last thing Gya felt like doing these days. She still hadn't bonded with Landon, and arrangements had been made with Bryant and his parents to have visitation with him. The Greens came to Gya's parents' home to spend time with their grandson, and Gya stayed in her room. Gya knew it was rude, but she couldn't muster the energy to fake pleasantries with them. She figured they assumed she was purposely avoiding them, given the ongoing divorce proceedings with their son. But things took a surprising turn at the beginning of November when Bryant visited alone. He'd just fed Landon and put him down for a nap, and he and Gya sat talking in her bedroom.

"Your mom has been worried about you, Gya. She revealed to me that you're suffering from postpartum depression, even though I figured things out on my own. I could tell you haven't been yourself. Look, I want to be here for you, Gigi." Gya couldn't remember the last time he'd called her by her pet name. "Do you still want to go through with this divorce? Landon needs the both of us. I don't want to parent him apart."

"In spite of all I'm going through, I'm willing to keep his best interests in mind and be amiable toward you," Gya said.

Bryant grabbed her hand and brought it to his lips, pressing a soft kiss against her knuckles. Gya's body seemed to betray her. Her heart rate increased as if she were having sharp heart palpitations. It intensified as she drew closer to him, stopping inches away from his moist lips. Bryant titled her chin and brought her lips into contact with his, and they shared a deep kiss. Gya was transported in time back to the first kiss they shared as college freshmen. Time stood still as they devoured each other's lips, but Gya finally pulled away with Bryant releasing a groan of protest.

"Come here, baby." Bryant gently pulled her back toward him and attempted to disrobe her.

Gya shook her head, refusing his further advances. "We've gone too far as it is. I'm sorry. I lost my head for a few minutes."

"Why are you apologizing? I'm your husband."

"Bryant, I'm not about to let you make love to me in my parents' home, not to mention with our son sleeping soundly just feet away."

"Yeah, I know I'll have you moaning loudly and wake him up. Now we wouldn't want that, would we?" Bryant said with a sly grin.

Gya couldn't help the grin and blush that emerged on her own face. She playfully pushed his shoulder. "Don't be crass. Now get out of here before you miss your flight back to Miami. Good luck with your upcoming game. Dad told me how you've been killing it out on the field."

"You and my son are my motivation, Gya. I'm not letting either of you go without a fight. I love you," Bryant said. He gave her a parting kiss before leaving the house.

Gya sat on her bed in a daze. She couldn't believe she was about to get down and dirty in her parents' house with the man she was so sure she hated mere months ago. Even now her body still emanated with desire, and a part of her wished they'd gotten intimate. She wondered if being overly amorous was a side effect of the antidepressant she'd been taking, although it hadn't been listed in the literature her doctor had given her.

Yeah, it had to be the medication because there was no way she was falling hard for her husband again. Was she?

Chapter Seventeen

Tatum had consistently been in prayer on King's behalf since he'd returned from Boston. He'd immediately retreated to their bedroom, which was where he spent most of his time lounging around in a spacey haze as he awaited the fate of his NBA career.

It came as no surprise that Kelsea called Tatum shortly after the brawl, lamenting about Antoine's arrest, fine, and impending suspension. "Do you realize the world of trouble King has gotten Antoine into?"

"Kelsea, Antoine is a grown man. No one forced him to run into the stands, but I must say I commend him for standing up for King. That's what a *real* friend would do, and it's much more than you have been to me."

"King has become nothing but a liability to the Flash, and I hope the rumors I'm hearing of him being banned from the league are true. He doesn't deserve to ever put on any NBA uniform again."

"Well, I'm glad that's not your call to make," Tatum scoffed.

"Whatever, Tatum. Continue to defend your husband who's nothing but a nuisance and menace to society. I want him to stay the hell away from Antoine for the rest of his pathetic life."

"With pleasure," Tatum said before hanging up in Kelsea's face.

The seemingly long-awaited press conference from the NBA commissioner finally arrived. Antoine and the other starting players were suspended for six months, which was half of the season. This came as joyous news for the players who sat on the bench for most games because the coaches were now forced to have to play them in the starting lineup since the star players were now suspended. As expected, King received the harshest punishment. While he wasn't banned from the NBA, he was suspended from playing for the remainder of the season. Following the press conference, sports pundits began to weigh in and speculate that the Flash would trade King since he'd become an occupational hazard to their franchise. The Flash fans weighed in on social media as well, citing that all chances of winning a team championship were now lost with all of the star players on suspension. Many die-hard fans were now out for King's blood, blaming him and his temper for extinguishing their chances at a championship ring. Social media was blazing with commentary such as King losing his temper gave further credence that he was guilty of the rape, and the wrath he displayed toward the disrespectful fan was the same fury in which he forced himself upon his rape victim.

Tatum now feared for her and King's safety, so she stayed indoors as much as possible and even took a hiatus from her TikTok and YouTube platforms.

But she was now worried about their financial future. Thankfully, the contract King signed with the Flash was guaranteed and couldn't be rescinded given his suspension, but what if the rumors about King being traded turned out to be true? What were his chances of being picked up by another team given his sullied character and reputation? With their daughter scheduled to make her arrival soon, Tatum now wished more than ever that she and King had stayed at UCLA and completed their college degrees. Perhaps King would've been a bit more mature and not made such foolish decisions that would land him in these huge controversies. And having degrees would've given him and Tatum career options to fall back on. Instead, their financial forecast now hung in the balance, and in Tatum's eyes, it looked rather bleak.

Chapter Eighteen

Gya's last encounter with Bryant still had her mind doing mental gymnastics. Stubborn as ever, she didn't want to cave and admit she still had strong feelings for him and was reconsidering the divorce. She'd even begun tuning in to his games again. He was a dominating force on the field and was a hot topic of reports on *SportsCenter* and other sports shows given his stellar performance on the field. As the holiday season neared, the Waves were still undefeated.

Meanwhile, Hannah and Shawn stepped down from their church amid reports of tax fraud and evasion on behalf of the multiple businesses they created outside of their ministry. The attorney general of the state of Georgia was closing in and conducting a full investigation. Gya couldn't help but feel smug that Hannah was finally receiving her comeuppance. Lauryn Roberts, messy as ever, had reached out to Gya repeatedly requesting she come onto her show to give her side of the story. Her inquiries went ignored, and Gya finally blocked her on all of her social media pages. God saw to it that Hannah was humbled, and Gya didn't feel the need to defend herself or heap more dirt on Hannah's name with all she'd uncovered from the PI. Her main concern was trying to sort out her conflicting emotions about the state of her marriage.

***

Tatum and King remained in the isolation of their home as they'd received reports from team personnel that several death threats had been made toward King for the demise of the Flash season. Tatum couldn't believe the sports idolatry of some "fans." She tried to keep it together for the sake of their child, but Tatum was under severe emotional duress as she feared for their well-being. She didn't like the idea of being caged inside of her own home, and she thought about how King's former lover Ireland had managed to make it past security and confront her at their front door. How did she know some deranged and twisted fan wouldn't manage to do the same? Their building security team assured her they were on high alert and on the lookout for any suspicious activity.

64

Tatum sat in their den watching a movie on Netflix to try and keep her mind occupied while King napped in their bedroom. Sleeping was all he seemed to do nowadays, and Tatum was worried that he was slowly slipping into a state of depression. Once the movie concluded, she waddled into their bedroom to find their bed empty. The bathroom door was closed, but she could see the light on inside. Tatum got into their bed and prepared to turn in for the night, but since entering her final trimester, she could never find a comfortable sleeping position. Minutes passed, and Tatum noticed she didn't hear any movement or running water from the bathroom.

"King?" she called out.

No answer.

Frowning, Tatum pushed back the blankets and got up to waddle over to the bathroom door. She tried to turn the knob and found it locked. She knocked. "King?" she called again.

Still no answer.

Tatum began to frantically pound on the door and call King's name. He never responded. With trembling hands, she grabbed her cell phone to dial 9-1-1. Her voice shook just as hard as she informed the dispatcher that her husband was locked away in their bathroom and unresponsive.

"How do you know he's unresponsive if you can't get inside?"

Tatum rolled her eyes, as she felt the dispatcher was being obtuse. "I mean he's not responding to me calling his name. Please send someone over quickly. I'm afraid he may be hurt. I don't know if he's collapsed or what. Please help."

"The police are en route," the dispatcher assured her.

King had still not emerged from the bathroom when the police arrived. They too pounded on the door and announced themselves, requesting that King come out. Tatum hoped she hadn't made a mistake by calling the police. What if King feared he'd be arrested again? Tatum's heart pounded furiously with fear and trepidation. She thought of all of the pill bottles that lined their medicine cabinet—medication that had been prescribed for King's various sports injuries. Medications that Tatum had once contemplated consuming in order to escape the nightmare of their relationship. She hadn't succumbed to the temptation, but had King? Was her husband laying on their bathroom floor unconscious from an intentional overdose? Or worse yet, already dead?

"Stand back," one of the officers ordered. He then kicked the door in.

Tatum released an anguished scream as her fears were confirmed. King was sprawled out on his back on the bathroom floor, his eyes closed, and the pallor of his skin a pasty gray. A couple of empty orange prescription pill bottles rested beside him.

"Noooo," Tatum wailed, sobbing uncontrollably. One of the policemen radioed for an ambulance while the other immediately began CPR on King.

"Lord, please save my husband," Tatum said, sobbing as she looked on helplessly.

***

The Lord was faithful as King was revived and transported to the hospital where his stomach was successfully pumped. He was taken into recovery so he could rest. Tatum was also admitted due to her blood pressure skyrocketing. She managed to make phone calls to her mother and King's family who made plans to fly in to New York City immediately.

Doctors made the decision to induce Tatum's labor, given she was only two weeks away from her scheduled delivery date. Tatum requested that the procedure take place once all of their family had arrived, as she didn't want to give birth alone. The following morning, Alani Nicole Watts was born.

Michelle was teary eyed as she held her granddaughter for the first time. "It's so bittersweet. Hopefully, your birth will give your daddy a renewed sense of purpose," Michelle cooed to Alani.

It was indeed a bittersweet moment, as King had missed out on the birth of his first child due to still being groggy. His father, Jacoby, was of little help and support, as he kept shaking his head in disbelief. "I can't believe King tried to take his own life. The son I raised is much stronger than that."

Tatum tuned out his nonsensical ramblings and nestled her newborn daughter to her bosom, placing a soft, gentle kiss upon her. In spite of the horrible circumstances surrounding her birth, Tatum felt her daughter was her world and couldn't wait to lavish her with all of the love and nurturing she deserved.

Chapter Nineteen

Gya resolved to pull herself out of her funk and be a more active parent to Landon. She also tried to get into the holiday spirit by making the decision to host Thanksgiving at her parents' home, even graciously extending an invite to Bryant and his family since the Waves had no game scheduled for Thanksgiving Day. Gya made a quick trip to New York City to see Alani for the first time, as well as to be a support for Tatum as she dealt with King's ordeal on top of becoming a new mother. Social media and sporting news channels had been rather brutal with their coverage of King's attempted suicide, citing that he was seeking to take the cowardly way out and he'd merely succumbed to his guilt for the rape. People's thoughts and opinions never ceased to amaze Gya, as humanity could be so cruel. Gya discussed as much with Bryant after their Thanksgiving meal as he lay Landon down for a nap.

"I promise you, Bryant, it seems like both Tatum and I have been embroiled in spiritual warfare since you and King went pro," Gya said as she bent to lay a soft kiss upon Landon's forehead as he slumbered in his crib.

Bryant stepped forward and gently brushed a strand of hair out of Gya's face, tucking it behind her ear before planting a soft kiss upon her cheek. "I know, baby, and if you'll allow me, I want to spend the rest of my life making it up to you. All I need is another chance, but hey...there's something I've been meaning to ask you. Why haven't you been going to church anymore?"

"Given the foolishness with Hannah, I've just become turned off by organized religion."

"Wow. Never thought I'd hear that from you, especially when I felt like I was competing against the church when we first got married."

Gya looked at him, her eyes full of surprise. "What do you mean?"

"I just felt this pressure to be perfect. You had this entire holy image to uphold, and so did I by default. My mind went into a whirlwind when Mercedes told me she was pregnant. I was so scared, Gya, not only of hurting you, but of what my infidelity coming to light meant for your brand. Sure, pro athletes get caught up in cheating all of the time, but once you throw God into the mix, it's a full-blown scandal, and that's exactly what happened."

"So you're saying you're glad I'm no longer super-religious or spiritual?"

"No, not at all. I want you to go to church again, but just not with all of the...zeal, I guess."

"Wait. Is this moreso about you or me?"

"Both. I'm done with being selfish. I have your best interests and well-being in mind just as much as my own, but I don't want Landon growing up with that kind of pressure to be perfect either. I know he'll already grow up with people expecting him to follow in my footsteps and be a football great. I don't want religious pressure on him as well," Bryant explained.

Gya nodded in understanding, and Bryant stood directly in front of her, capturing her lips within his for a deep, sultry kiss, which Gya eagerly returned. She couldn't blame the medication this time around. Her heart was yielding toward her husband, and she felt herself falling for him all over again. But there was still the question of his daughter, Brelynn. Could Gya ever put her resentment aside and accept her?

***

Thanksgiving was uneventful in New York City for Tatum and King. Her mother, Vanessa, had temporarily moved in to help Tatum adjust to motherhood and care for Alani, as well as nursing King back to health mentally. Tatum wasn't in any celebratory mood anyhow, feeling the only thing she had to be thankful for was the birth of her child. And a part of her was angry with King, finding his suicide attempt rather selfish. She couldn't believe he was willing to leave her as a single mother and Alani fatherless. And after their catered Thanksgiving meal from Sylvia's of Harlem, Tatum decided to have a come-to-Jesus moment with King about her feelings. Since being released from the hospital and placed on antidepressant medication, King had walked around the house like a zombie, his eyes lifeless and sometimes glazed.

"King, I just want to understand where your head was on that night. Did you not care enough about me or Alani before trying to check out of here?"

"I wasn't thinking of anything that night other than wanting the pain to go away. I've lost everything. I guess I didn't think twice about how you would feel to lose me, and for that I apologize. I mean, besides you and my family, everyone else has turned on me. You even lost your friendship with Kelsea because of me."

Tatum sucked her teeth. "I didn't lose anything with her because she proved she was never my friend to begin with." It wasn't surprising that Kelsea didn't call to offer any form of solace concerning King's ordeal or to congratulate Tatum on her new addition, although her husband, Antoine, did. Tatum noticed King's eyelids fluttering, so she let him rest, as frequent naps was another side effect of his medication.

As she straightened up the kitchen and put away leftovers from their dismal Thanksgiving feast, she mulled on how her twenty-third birthday was the following week. And it felt like a bout with depression was the only gift she'd receive. This was not how she envisioned the start of motherhood, as it was a struggle to make it from one day to the next, but she was determined to start seeing a therapist, and King was ordered by his doctor to start weekly therapy sessions as well. It was a condition he agreed to in order to be released from the hospital, instead of being transferred to the psychiatric ward. King had been consistent with his appointments, and Tatum felt she owed it to her daughter to take care of herself mentally too. She couldn't fight off the feeling that both she and King were failing their daughter, having her born into such controversies, but Tatum resolved to do her best to turn things around for the better within her life and marriage.

Chapter Twenty

The revamping of King's image was underway, and his publicist Kimberly suggested that King record an apology for the brawl that would be shared on social media and sent to several sporting news outlets. Tatum and Alani would also be present within the video, with their fireplace lit and a fully decorated Christmas tree displayed in their background. King would also apologize to the man he assaulted, as a hefty settlement had been reached and the guy agreed to drop all charges. He would conclude the video with holiday well wishes. Kimberly insisted that giving the public an exclusive first look at Baby Alani would soften their hearts and help cultivate King's former bad-boy image into one of a mature and responsible family man. Tatum brokered no argument and agreed to follow Kimberly's directives, though she was a bit insecure about the lingering weight gain incurred from her pregnancy.

King's agent felt that a trade from New York City was inevitable at this point and was putting out feelers with different teams to gauge interest. He hoped the video of apology would work in King's favor in getting team owners to take a chance on him. Tatum was in prayer for the same. Her birthday was just as uneventful as their Thanksgiving, given that she and King had a quiet and intimate dinner at home while their mother looked after Alani in another room. She embraced the idea of King being traded away from the Flash and pondered the different cities in which she'd like to relocate. Her hometown of Houston was a start, and she shared with King that she'd like him to consider playing for the Houston Asteroids, although he was considering playing in his hometown of Memphis. King felt he had a better chance of being welcomed by the city he'd grown up in.

***

Meanwhile, back in Houston, Gya's mom was trying to convince her to attend church for the upcoming watch night service on New Year's Eve, but Gya was still reluctant.

"Besides, Bryant wants Landon and I to spend Christmas in Miami with him. I'm strongly considering it, Mom, and staying until after the New Year."

Pam smiled knowingly. "I'm not surprised. I caught the vibe between you two on Thanksgiving. So am I to assume that you are officially reconciling?"

"Nothing is official just yet, but I am considering bringing a halt to the divorce proceedings," Gya said, then she groaned. "People are going to think I'm one big fool."

"You can't worry about the opinions of others. You do what you feel is best for you and Landon. I'm here to support you either way, and I know your father feels the same."

"I'm glad that stupid show *Sidepieces* won't be renewed for another season due to low ratings. It was such a silly concept to begin with, and I'm glad most of the viewing public had enough brain cells to realize infidelity shouldn't be glamorized," Gya said.

She didn't voice her concerns aloud, but Gya wondered if Mercedes would try to sink her claws into Bryant even harder now that the show had been cancelled, as she was nothing but a gold digger and saw him as a mere meal ticket. This also gave her pause on wanting to reconcile with Bryant because as the mother of his daughter, she'd forever be a source of contention. She imagined that Mercedes' presence in their lives would be just as annoying as a bloodthirsty mosquito. Gya had to ask herself if it was all worth it.

Chapter Twenty-one

Tatum suggested that King's family fly in and spend Christmas with them, staying for two weeks before returning to Memphis after the new year. Vanessa had flown back to Houston, eager to spend the Christmas holiday with a guy she'd been seeing for over a year. Vanessa mentioned she was anxious for him to propose and felt comfortable with accepting, as she was now certain he was not a clout chaser.

Tatum felt that King's family being at their home would help brighten his spirits, and she was right. They enjoyed a warm, festive Christmas. For New Year's Eve, Tatum planned a family game night, topped by a toast at midnight, although King and his father, Jacoby, started drinking much earlier into the evening. Tatum had her concerns about King drinking alcohol while on antidepressant medication, but the mood was so bright that she didn't want to nag him. But things soon took a turn for the worse when Jacoby went on a drunken tirade against King's youngest brother, Korey.

"Can you believe Korey wanted to bring his boyfriend along?" Jacoby said as he looked at the cards in his hand.

They were all engaged in a game of spades, which had gotten rather animated and loud with trash talk. Tatum had to warn them to lower their voices so as not to awaken Alani, who was slumbering peacefully in her crib in another room.

"Dad, I don't know why you were even tripping off that," Korey defended. "Mom has accepted Darius, so I don't see why you can't. This is who I am, and I'm not changing for anyone."

"Dad isn't the only one tripping. You didn't ask me if you could bring another dude to my home. I would've said no," King said firmly.

"That's my *boy*," Jacoby said with a smirk in King's direction.

"Jacoby, let's not go in this direction. This has been a nice night and holiday overall. Let's not ruin it," King's mother, Michelle, intervened.

"But that's just it, Mom," Korey insisted. "Why is discussing my sexuality such a touchy topic with them?"

"'Cause it's unnatural, *boy,* and you know what else is unnatural? Being jealous of your own brother," Jacoby roared.

"What? I'm not jealous of King," Korey shot back.

"Then why did you get that Whitney girl to set him up and accuse him of rape?" Jacoby demanded.

Tatum felt her heart drop, and she released a gasp of shock, her eyes darting wildly in Korey's direction for an explanation.

King dropped his cards. "What the hell, Korey?"

"Dad, that's a damn lie," Korey said.

"You left your phone on the kitchen counter at home one afternoon and imagine how shocked I was when I saw that she was calling your phone. For you to actually have her saved as a contact let me know y'all have been in touch for awhile. I also read the text messages you two exchanged." Jacoby said.

"See, that's what you get for jumping to conclusions. *I'm* the one that convinced her to drop the case," Korey defended.

"Why the hell were you even talking to her in the first place?" King demanded.

"King, in spite of how you shun me, you're still my brother, and I love you. I never believed you raped that girl. I reached out to her on your behalf and pleaded with her to drop the charges and settle instead."

"Dad, what did the texts say?" King asked.

"From what I remember, Korey asked if she'd done what he told her to," Jacoby responded.

"Exactly. I was talking about her telling her lawyer she wanted to drop the case," Korey said, exasperated.

Tatum's heart was beating rapidly, but Korey's story sounded plausible. After all, she'd also tracked Whitney's information down through the PI she'd hired. It wasn't farfetched for Korey to have done the same.

"And anyway, I'm not the only one keeping secrets in this family. Dad, since you're running off at the mouth, tell Mom all about the nine-year-old son you fathered behind her back. King, did you know we have a younger brother?" Korey revealed.

Tatum heard Michelle's sharp intake of breath.

King frowned. "What?"

"Yeah, that's right. Dad had an affair on Mom. That must be where you get your philandering ways from," Korey said.

King swallowed and looked at his father questioningly. "Dad, is this true?"

"You selfish bastard. Why would you go and hurt your mom like this?" Jacoby raged at Korey.

"You're one to talk. You and King are two of the most selfish people in this family, and you're the one who hurt her with your lies, not me," Korey said.

"Dad, I don't believe this," King said, looking at his father in disappointment.

"Yeah? Well, you're also not going to believe that your precious wife knew, too, and used the information to blackmail me. She pressured me into getting you to marry her without a prenup or else she was going to tell you and your mother," Jacoby said, glaring at Tatum.

King's head whipped in Tatum's direction. "Tay? Is that true?"

"King, I was only bluffing. I wouldn't dare hurt you or Miss Michelle like that."

"Oh, but you did, and it was no bluff," Jacoby said.

"King, baby, I promise I would've signed the prenup. I was just upset at the way Jacoby talked to me after what went down with the sports reporter," Tatum defended herself, referring to the incident last December where she'd slapped a female sports reporter after mistakenly thinking she was another one of King's lovers.

Michelle was crying softly, and King went to console her.

"I–I'm sorry, Mom. Please don't cry," Korey said, going toward his mother.

"Stay the hell away from her. I want you out of my house," King fumed at his brother. "And you too, Dad. I'm firing you as my manager. I can't believe you would hurt my mother like this. And Korey, I'm done with you too. I'm still not fully convinced that you didn't scheme with Whitney to set me up."

Korey's eyes filled with tears.

"No need for your father to leave. I'm going back to Memphis. I need to get as far away from you as possible," Michelle said, shooting daggers at her husband as she spoke. "I don't want him at the house. I plan to file for divorce. This is unforgiveable, Jacoby."

King glanced over at Tatum. "So this marriage was nothing but a cash grab for you?"

"King, you know that's not true. Otherwise, I wouldn't have stayed throughout this rape fiasco. Can't you see it's because I truly love you?"

"No woman who loves me would blackmail my father and threaten to break my mother's heart. You harbored a secret that would tear my family apart, and you used money as leverage. Like my mom said, that's unforgiveable," King said.

"Unforgiveable?" Tatum choked out. "Do you know how many times I've forgiven *you* since we've been together? The cheating, the STD, the rape, the brawl. I stood by your side through it all, but you're telling me you can't forgive me?"

Michelle stood silently and left the room. Korey stalked into the guest room to begin packing his things.

"Dad, I don't know why you're still sitting here. I meant it when I said I want you out of here and out of my life," King said firmly.

"Son," Jacoby said, walking toward King.

"Leave," King barked.

With his head hung low, Jacoby stood and silently went to gather his belongings.

"I'm going to return to Memphis with my mom. I need some space to think about everything," King said to Tatum once they were alone.

"So you're seriously going to up and leave me, King? What about Alani?"

"Like I said, Tatum, everything shared on tonight is a lot to unpack. I need space to make sense of all this. You betrayed me. Even if you didn't tell my mom, you could've at least told me. I can't believe you harbored this secret for so long."

"Because I knew it would hurt you, King. I know you once thought the world of your dad."

"And I once thought the world of you too," King said.

He then left the room, leaving Tatum to stare after him, speechless, in his wake.

Chapter Twenty-two

Though Gya didn't yield to her mother's request to attend watch night service on New Year's Eve, she spent the evening having a quiet and intimate dinner with Bryant in a secluded section of The Capital Grille restaurant in Miami.

"Talk about a full circle moment, huh?" Gya said as she sipped from a glass of red wine.

Bryant had raised an eyebrow when she requested the Cabernet Sauvignon, remarking that he never thought he'd see the day on which she'd drink something stronger than water. Gya had picked up a bottle of wine a few weeks ago while at the supermarket, and she loved how it relaxed and soothed her nerves. She preferred a glass of wine as opposed to the antidepressant medication, which was why she discontinued taking it. But Gya was careful to drink in moderation, as she didn't want alcoholism to sneak up on her.

"Full circle?" Bryant questioned as he perused the menu.

"Yeah. This same time last year we were reconnecting and trying to move past the adultery, and now here we are again...on the same page. Bryant, I'm scared. How do I know this time will be different?" Gya said in a surprising moment of vulnerability and transparency.

Bryant took her hand and brought it to his soft, moist lips, kissing it soothingly. Where Gya had once recoiled from his touch, it now caused her to imagine melting to the floor in a puddle of chocolate "Because I love you so much. We're both parents now, and we have to be willing to grow and move forward for the kids. And that's something else I wanted to talk to you about tonight." Bryant took a deep breath. "I want to file for full custody of Brelynn."

Gya swallowed, her breathing measured. She wasn't anticipating this bit of news.

"I know it's a lot to ask of you, but I don't feel Mercedes has Brelynn's best interests in mind. She's young and likes to party all of the time and take all of these exotic vacations. Brelynn is nothing but a paycheck to her. She's not mature enough to handle motherhood," Bryant revealed.

Gya nodded in understanding.

"But what does this mean for us and our reconciliation? Can you handle welcoming Brelynn into our family? And if not, I love you to life, Gya, but I have no choice but to let you go. Brelynn is my daughter, and I can't shut her out just to appease you."

Gya couldn't explain it, but her heart warmed at hearing Bryant say those words. He was willing to let her go just so he could be a responsible father to his daughter, and she admired that.

"And it was selfish of me to expect you to. Yes, Bryant, I'm willing to work past any resentment and welcome Brelynn into our fold."

Bryant exhaled and a megawatt smile came across his handsome features. He leaned across the table and planted a kiss upon Gya's full lips. "I love you, woman."

"And I'm learning to love you more again," Gya said.

"I've been keeping documentation of Mercedes' actions for the courts as my attorney advised. I know we have an uphill battle before us. Mercedes will try to use my NFL schedule against me being an active and attentive parent, along with trying to paint you as a wicked stepmother given the circumstances of the affair. I just want to know you're by my side for the long haul."

"I'm here, Bryant. I mean, after all we've already been through, I'd say we can weather any storm or test at this point in the game," Gya said confidently.

"The game plan was for my folks to move to Miami to help me care for Brelynn, but that was before we made our reconciliation official. So just when do you plan to move back?" Bryant asked.

"Landon and I can make the move sometime at the beginning of the year," Gya confirmed.

She'd actually fallen in love with the city of Miami and missed it. She couldn't wait to live near the beautiful scenic ocean views once again.

Bryant released a smile of relief. "And I can hardly wait. Man, God is so faithful. Still in the midst of an undefeated season, and now I have my wife and family back. Even if we don't win the Super Bowl, I've already won the biggest and best blessing of all."

Gya smiled, and they brought in the new year with a toast to their reconciled love, sealing their recommitment with a long, sultry kiss.

***

Gya wasn't the only one on the move for the new year. Tatum made the decision to move back to Los Angeles and complete her final year of school at UCLA. She was still debating on whether to complete school online or attend classes in person, although given Alani, the former option seemed like the best bet. But Tatum also wanted to interview nannies once she was settled into LA. Her mother, Vanessa, returned to New York City to help her pack up the apartment, which King had listed for sale. Tatum couldn't believe how he'd refused to speak to her since the New Year's Eve fiasco, totally freezing her out. Tatum was expecting to be served with divorce papers at any moment, and she decided she wouldn't contest. She'd gladly sign, as King had proven that he was nothing but a selfish and narcissistic bastard. She was livid at how he was icing out Alani when she was the innocent party in the entire situation. Her daughter didn't deserve a father who was a deadbeat, which was what King was shaping up to be.

By the end of January, Tatum and Alani were all moved in to a beautiful high-rise apartment in LA that offered a great view of the city, just as the New York City apartment, and was a mere block away from the Staples Center. She reasoned that if King came to his senses and had the good fortune of being picked up by another NBA team, then he'd be in close proximity to visit with Alani whenever he had a game in LA.

Tatum still kept in touch with Korey who was now estranged from everyone except for his mother, Michelle, who kept him abreast of family happenings. She'd officially filed for divorce from Jacoby who had now moved in with the mother of his nine-year old son, although Korey reasoned that this woman was nothing but a rebound and Jacoby was just using her for a place to stay. He also told Tatum that King's publicist was having him do charity work with the Make-A-Wish Foundation. His agent was also in talks with the Memphis Grizzlies, who were considering signing King. In spite of it all, Tatum wished King the best and hoped he'd be able to salvage his NBA career and ingratiate himself into the public's good graces once again. But her main focus was finishing her degree and embarking on a new life as a single mother, and she prayed daily for God's grace to be upon her and Alani every step of the way.

Chapter Twenty-three

The Miami Waves were headed to the Super Bowl against the defending champions, the Kansas City Chiefs, and Bryant was named the National Football League's Offensive Player of the Year. Gya was ecstatic for him, as he'd had regrets about missing out on winning the Rookie of the Year honor due to an injury that had cut his first season short. Though Gya was still kind of iffy when it came to religion, she couldn't deny evidence of God's faithfulness continually at work.

She and Landon had officially moved back to Miami. The Super Bowl was held in LA, so she and Landon spent time visiting with Tatum and Alani during the weekend of the big game. Tatum was taking classes online and would complete her degree by December.

"You know I could just as easily go to summer school and be finished by then. But I got an offer I wanted to run by you for some advice," Tatum said. She revealed that Entertainment Central network had reached out to her and offered her a hosting and commentating gig. The executives had viewed her online content and liked her energy, feeling she would be a great asset to their network doing award show interviews and red carpet events.

"I'm very interested in accepting, especially given that I'm pursuing a degree in mass communications, and I like the idea of carving my own path outside of King. I need to know what this means for Alani because a great deal of travel is involved. The network said I could take her along with me, and of course she has the nanny I hired. I just don't want her to ever feel neglected, and I refuse to put a career over her best interests—I mean she's only a few months old."

"I feel where you're coming from, but I think you're overanalyzing everything. It's great that the network will accommodate you bringing her on the road. I feel you should take the offer. No one will label you as a bad parent for having a career," Gya encouraged.

"Thanks, cousin. I guess given King's abandonment, I'm just overprotective of Alani."

"Hopefully, he'll see the error of his ways and eventually come around," Gya said.

"You know, I really like this new you—sound advice without all of the judgment and criticism," Tatum said.

Gya threw a pillow from the sofa in her direction, and they both shared a laugh. Tatum asked how things were going with the reconciliation, and Gya revealed Bryant's plans to file for full custody of Brelynn.

"I'm glad you're onboard with it. Like I said, after King's behavior, I don't want to see another innocent child shunned by their father. Bryant is having one helluva season, and I can't wait for the big game. You think they'll pull off a win again Kansas City?"

"I sure hope so, cousin, or the media will never let the Waves live the Super Bowl loss down after coming off an undefeated season," Gya mulled.

***

The Super Bowl game was a close one, but the Waves were able to win the championship by a field goal. The Miami Waves were the second team in NFL history to have an undefeated season, making for a big celebration in the city of Miami. Bryant was also crowned as the game's Most Valuable Player and chosen for the Disney World "What's Next?" commercial that aired every year following the big game in which he smiled into the camera with his pearly whites and proclaimed the infamous line of "I'm going to Disney World."

But of course, where there is happiness, drama is not too far behind. Gya knew Mercedes would be a source of contention upon her decision to reconcile with Bryant, and Mercedes didn't disappoint. Bryant wanted Brelynn to accompany them to Disney World, as the reigning Super Bowl champs were treated to sponsored trips to the resort each year. But Mercedes, determined to be difficult, asked to come along as well. Bryant told her no, as it was disrespectful to Gya. Mercedes argued that she didn't trust Gya or trust Bryant's family to be alone with her child and insisted she needed to come along. Bryant again refused, so Mercedes told him unless she could come, then Brelynn wouldn't be allowed to come either.

She also became irate because Brelynn wasn't invited to ride on the parade bus during the Miami Waves victory celebration in downtown Miami, joining Bryant, Gya, and the rest of the Waves players and their families. Bryant pointed out how Landon wasn't present either, as Gya's mother had flown in

80

and babysat for them during the city celebration, but Mercedes wasn't having it. She felt that Bryant purposefully excluded her daughter, and the only reason Landon wasn't present for the parade was due to him only being a few months old.

Gya felt Mercedes had a lot of nerve in trying to impart a sister wives arrangement. Including Brelynn within their family did not apply to her and Gya found her behavior to be immature and foolish.

But Mercedes wouldn't let the issue rest. She took to social media to tell the world how Bryant and Gya were rejecting her daughter now that they'd reconciled. She chronicled how they didn't allow Brelynn to come to the victory parade nor accompany them on the family trip to Disney World, conveniently leaving out how she wouldn't let Brelynn go unless she was included. There was a divide of opinions, with some bashing Gya and Bryant, while others faulted Mercedes for having a child by a married man, citing that she birthed Brelynn at a disadvantage, which wasn't fair to her.

Gya and Bryant were determined not to let the social media frenzy get under their skin this time around. Mercedes' antics were further documentation to use against her in court, as Bryant planned to file the suit for full custody soon.

Meanwhile, there was another love triangle that had social media in an uproar. Shawn filed for divorce from Hannah, and he was now involved with their nanny Erinn. He also shuttered the doors on their church, The Living Word. Shawn went on *The Lauryn Roberts Show* and revealed that he was never called to pastor in the first place and only did it because other male ministers said it was out of order for Hannah to be leading a church. Shawn felt within his heart that God told him that their nanny Erinn was his true soulmate. He loved how good she was with the children he shared with Hannah and couldn't wait for them to wed and start a family of their own. It was then that Shawn spilled all and told the world about how Hannah had never given birth to any children. The backlash against Hannah was fierce, and she was run out of Atlanta in shame.

When it was all said and done, Gya was glad that she wasn't the one to reveal the truth about Hannah, as everything about her double life had come to the forefront. Gya acknowledged that God had a way of righting all wrongs and bringing the truth to light.

Chapter Twenty-four

Tatum could hardly believe her eyes and ears as she watched the filmed footage obtained by TMZ of King's accuser, Whitney Prescott, confessing to lying about the rape.

"I'm telling you, what they say about black dudes being hung is not a myth. King was one of the greatest screws of my life," Whitney boasted. Her words were a bit slurred as she was obviously intoxicated. The full-length video was about five minutes long, but the news media had taken the most salacious soundbites to share with the public.

"So why'd you accuse him of rape?" said a voice off camera, which was the voice of one of Whitney's male friends. This male friend was down on his luck and recorded Whitney with the intent of selling the video to tabloids.

"For a free and easy payday. Have you seen my student loan debt? And this is only my junior year. But I had no intention of ever going through with the trial, even before King's brother contacted me asking me to show mercy to his big brother by accepting a settlement. He had no idea that was my end goal all along, but I wanted King to be desperate enough to give a hefty settlement, which is why I waited so long to drop the case," Whitney said.

Now that she worked for Entertainment Central, Tatum had been tipped off about the video before the news was shared with the public. Once TMZ posted the video, it had nearly broken the internet. Whitney was arrested and charged with filing a false criminal complaint, and King had his name cleared. In spite of everything, Tatum was happy for King. Of course, the news media had done a complete one-eighty and was now painting King as a victim of entrapment who'd been falsely accused and taken advantage of.

Tatum released a long exhale, glad that the rape debacle could be put behind them. She hoped Whitney would get everything that was coming to her. Her treacherous actions had made her life a living hell for all of those months, and it had all been because of a filthy lie. The fallout from that one accusation had been tremendous, but Tatum asked that God help her to forgive and move forward. King still had yet to file for divorce, so Tatum decided to make the first move and would file the paperwork the following week.

But for now, she needed to get her head on straight, as tonight was her first official hosting gig, which was the red carpet premiere of Issa Rae's newest series. Tatum was slated to interview all cast and attendees about topics ranging from what designer they were wearing to their thoughts about the new show. And Tatum had the pleasure of interviewing the suave and debonair Jamarcus Jackson, an older NBA legend who was forced to retire from the league over a decade before due to colon cancer. But it was a battle he fought and won, as he'd since been in remission and was now a stellar businessman and philanthropist with numerous ventures. His production company had partnered with Issa to bring forth the new series.

Tatum could hardly concentrate, as she found Jamarcus' baritone voice and the scent of his cologne so alluring. Tatum licked her lips as he spoke, and she felt her womanly parts quake as he gave her slim, svelte figure a once-over with his dark, penetrating eyes.

"I'll catch up with you after the show," Jamarcus said with a wink.

Goodness, I hope so, Tatum thought but gave him a big smile and wave in return. She couldn't believe she was lusting after a man twice her age. But given King's juvenile behavior, perhaps a sugar daddy was just what she needed in her life.

***

Gya had just put Landon down for a nap and was in the kitchen preparing a sandwich when she heard the doorbell. Whoever was outside kept pressing down on the buzzer like a maniac.

Gya went to the front door, her attractive features set in annoyance, which deepened when she saw the visitor on the other side of the door, none other than Mercedes herself.

Mercedes stormed into the house like a banshee once Gya opened the door. Though their neighborhood was gated, Mercedes had the access code. Bryant had provided her with it for the times when she'd dropped off Brelynn for visitation. Now she'd taken it upon herself to just drop in unannounced, which Gya would make certain to talk to Bryant about later. Boundaries needed to be set and established now that they were back together.

"Where's Bryant?" Mercedes demanded, her dark brown eyes blazing.

"He's out on an errand, Mercedes. What can I help you with?"

"You can't help me with a damned thing, Little Miss Priss. Nah, I take that back. Tell me how the hell you and Bryant think you can try and take my child away from me?" Mercedes fumed as she followed Gya back into the kitchen.

Gya calmly resumed making her sandwich, using a knife to slide mayo on a piece of bread. She knew Mercedes would hit the roof once she received word of the filing.

"That's between you and Bryant, but I support him fully, and I want to assure you, you have nothing to worry about. I won't mistreat Brelynn in any form or fashion."

"Yeah, right. I know you hate her just as much as you hate me. I can't believe you went as far as wishing me dead, but I'm gonna show you who you're messing with," Mercedes said, coming to snatch the knife out of Gya's hand.

"Where's that little bastard, Landon? You think you're gonna take my child away from me? Let's see how you like me messing with yours," Mercedes said as she made a run for the direction of the stairs.

Gya's mama bear instincts went into full force, and she tackled Mercedes to the ground at the foot of the stairs. She and Mercedes then tussled for control of the knife. Mercedes bit Gya's wrist as Gya attempted to wrestle the knife out of her grip. Gya let out a yelp in pain and kicked at Mercedes who then continued on her mission to head upstairs, but Gya caught up with her, gripping her by the neck from behind. Mercedes swiped at Gya's hand to try and break loose, but Gya grabbed Mercedes by the hair. Mercedes continued to swipe at Gya with the knife, her head at an awkward angle from Gya's grip.

"You think you won 'cause Bryant came back to you, huh?" Mercedes rasped. "Did he tell you about all of the times we made love upstairs whenever I'd bring Brelynn to visit? He should be with me not you."

As if Gya's heart could beat any more rapidly, it accelerated at hearing Mercedes words. Was she telling the truth? Bryant had assured her he hadn't been with Mercedes or anyone else during their separation.

With a newfound strength, Gya let out an infuriated scream, flipping Mercedes onto her back. The sudden movement took Mercedes by complete surprise, and she dropped the knife. Both ladies made a dash for the weapon, but Gya was quicker. She grabbed the knife and straddled Mercedes, holding the knife up to her throat. "If I let you up, your next move should be to get out of this house. Do you understand me?" Gya said.

Mercedes raised her arms and wrapped both hands around Gya's throat. Gya then plunged the knife into Mercedes neck in an effort to break free from her grasp, but she nicked an artery and a thick stream of blood burst forth.

Both Gya's and Mercedes's eyes widened at the same time; Gya's in shock at what she'd done, and Mercedes in agonizing pain. Gya backed away in horror, looking at her bloodied hand in disbelief.

Gya's mind was spinning with fear and trepidation. She knew she had to call the police but where was her cell phone? No, first she needed to try and get the bleeding under control. Gya ran to the kitchen in search of a towel to hold against Mercedes' wound. When she returned, Mercedes was taking deep, labored breaths.

"Stay with me, Mercedes. Please stay with me," Gya gasped, her hands shaking uncontrollably as she pressed the towel against Mercedes' neck. The white towel immediately turned a cranberry red as it absorbed the blood flow.

Mercedes' eyelids fluttered, and her chest rose and fell one last time before she closed her eyes.

"Mercedes? Mercedes, nooooo..."

Stay tuned for Book 3: Interception.

Discussion Questions

1. What took place in *Interference* that surprised you the most?
2. How have the characters grown over the course of the series so far?
3. What surprised you most about what Gya uncovered about Hannah?
4. Did you agree with Gya's decision not to expose Hannah publicly? Why or why not?
5. Were you saddened by the demise of Kelsea and Tatum's friendship? Why or why not?
6. Were you always fully convinced of King's innocence?
7. Do you think Gya should have reconciled with Bryant or gone through with the divorce?
8. What are your thoughts about King leaving Tatum?
9. Are you hoping King and Tatum will reconcile? Why or why not?
10. Did Mercedes succumb to her injuries, or do you think she'll survive?

Don't miss out!

Visit the website below and you can sign up to receive emails whenever Sherron Elise publishes a new book. There's no charge and no obligation.

https://books2read.com/r/B-A-BGFT-NFDGC

BOOKS 2 READ

Connecting independent readers to independent writers.

Did you love *Interference*? Then you should read *All That Glitters*[1] by Sherron Elise!

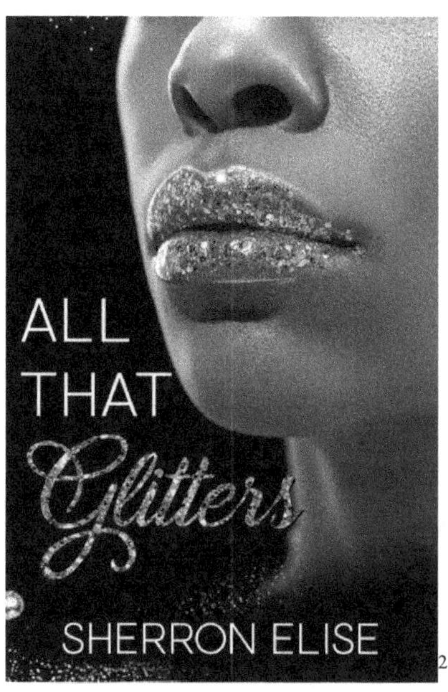

[2]

When her best friend lucks up and marries an NFL superstar, college senior Racquel Spencer sets out on a mission to find and wed a Mr. Money Bags of her own. Racquel is not above breaking rules, or hearts, to get what she desires. But she will learn that even the best laid plans have a tendency to backfire, and they will inadvertently explode in her M.A.C. powdered face.

18-year old Harmony Eubanks feels that college is a waste of time and just wants to become Houston's next R&B singing sensation. But when an opportunity at a life of stardom presents itself she will find that it also carries a lot of drama, hardship and even tragedy. These turn of events will force Harmony to face some hard truths about her life...and herself.

College freshman Skyye Reynolds has always carried a torch for NBA superstar Jarad Rolands. Her obsession with him dates back to the days when he was just a high school basketball phenom in her hometown. But things

---

1. https://books2read.com/u/3y1ExB

2. https://books2read.com/u/3y1ExB

become dangerous when the lines between fantasy and reality become blurred for Skyye, causing her world to spin out of control.

Raine Chambers is the youngest daughter of world renowned mega church founder, Bishop Lyndall Chambers. Being away at college for the first time means she's no longer under the watchful eyes of her father and mother. This newfound freedom prompts a curious and naïve Raine to test the waters of homosexuality and explore a relationship with another female. But becoming entangled in this act of rebellion against her spiritual beliefs will carry a high price tag. Raine's life spirals into disaster and places her family's stellar church reputation at risk.

Read more at https://sherronelise.com/.

About the Author

Sherron Elise is a proud native of Houston, Texas. An avid reader since childhood, her passion for getting lost within the pages of a book soon transformed into using her vivid imagination to create stories of her own. For more information about Sherron Elise you can visit her website at www.sherronelise.com and subscribe to her podcast, The College Christian Chat, available on Apple, Spotify, and other listening platforms.

Read more at https://sherronelise.com/.